# Hun for Hire

"Now then, Mrs. Guttman," Miles said gently. He paused and looked at the jury. "Could you tell us who David Gonzales is?"

Mrs. Guttman stopped sniffling and blinked at him apprehensively.

"Well . . ." she puckered her collagen lips as if trying to remember. "He's the tennis pro . . . at the club."

Miles sadly shook his head. "Ah ha . . ."

Both Mrs. Guttman and her lawyer stiffened as Miles reached back and Wrigley put a sheaf of papers in his hand. For a millimoment Wrigley felt as if he'd passed the sword to the matador. It was glorious.

"He's the tennis pro at the club," Miles said, voice steely cold as he lifted the papers. "Then why are your letters to him addressed 'Dear David and Goliath'?"

*Two jeweled ears and her tail,* Wrigley exulted in watching Mrs. Guttman's lawyer vainly plead with the judge. He was in the presence of greatness.

Miles took it all in stride. He packed up his briefcase, gave the jury a brilliant smile and was off to the next battle.

Attila the Hun would have been proud.

# INTOLERABLE CRUELTY

A novel by F.J. Lauria
Based on the motion picture story by
Robert Ramsey & Matthew Stone and John Romano
Screenplay by Robert Ramsey & Matthew Stone and Ethan Coen & Joel Coen

**POCKET STAR BOOKS**
New York London Toronto Sydney Singapore

An *Original* Publication of POCKET BOOKS

 A Pocket Star Book published by
POCKET BOOKS, a division of Simon & Schuster, Inc.
1230 Avenue of the Americas, New York, NY 10020

ISBN: 0-7434-7063-X

First Pocket Books printing October 2003

10  9  8  7  6  5  4  3  2  1

POCKET STAR BOOKS and colophon are registered trademarks of Simon & Schuster, Inc.

Manufactured in the United States of America

For information regarding special discounts for bulk purchases, please contact Simon & Schuster Special Sales at 1-800-456-6798 or business@simonandschuster.com

Whoever loved, who loved not at first sight?
—Miles Massey

# INTOLERABLE
# CRUELTY

# CHAPTER
## ONE

Donovan was in a nasty mood. His eleven o'clock production meeting had been canceled without notice. *Braverman*, he thought bitterly. A mental image of the pudgy, smirking associate producer made his stomach curl. Braverman was trying to sandbag him and take over the show. But the putz didn't know who he was dealing with. For he, Donovan Donnelly, the king of daytime TV, was going to cut off Braverman's balls and hang them beside his Emmys.

The visual comforted him as he eased the Jaguar off Rodeo Drive. He started to feel better as he neared the modest mansion he called home. He loved Beverly Hills; the palm trees, the carefully tended lawns, the trappings of wealth and power on display on every manicured lot. He was a lucky man. Top dog in a dog-eat-dog profession.

Donovan checked his reflection in the rearview. *Not bad for my age.* He stayed in shape, tennis three times a week despite a killer work schedule. Producing a top-rated soap opera like *The Sands of Time* was tough, demanding work.

*Fortunately I'm a tough, demanding sonuvabitch,* Donovan gloated, turning his head to admire his ponytail. Armando had done a superb job on his hair. Yes, life was good in good old Hollywood.

As Donovan neared home he was mildly surprised to see a bruised, dirty white panel truck squatting in his driveway like a dead elephant.

*Makes the house look third world,* Donovan fumed, slipping the Jag into the carport. Still glaring at the truck, he rolled out of the car and marched to the front door.

Before going inside he paused and read the ad attached to his doorknob.

OLLIE'LL FIX IT! the ad declared boldly but neglected to supply specifics. Donovan wondered what was broken.

Entering the house Donovan was greeted by the gurgling fountain in the center of the Italian tile foyer. He had chosen the tiles himself while honeymooning in Sardinia. He had even flown the tile maker to L.A. to supervise their installation.

But when he stepped inside Donovan saw that the aesthetic of the octagonal pattern was now marred by a pile of promotional literature heaped on the floor. He peered at the top layer. OLLIE'LL FIX IT!

*What the hell was broken?*

"Bonnie!" Donovan called, moving toward the long hall.

It took long seconds before he got a reply.

"Donovan . . . ?"

Bonnie's voice sounded very distant and very surprised.

*Probably in the bathroom,* he speculated. *She spends half the day in there.*

Turning the corner Donovan saw the door at the end of the hallway closing. It was the door to the den. His den.

The door to the master bedroom stood open.

". . . Bonnie?"

". . . Donovan?"

Bonnie's voice was still distant. Donovan scowled and marched to the end of the hall. As he passed the open door he glanced inside. There was no sign of Bonnie but the bed was rumpled.

A queasy sensation began churning inside Donovan's belly. He tried the door at the end of the hall. The one he had just seen close shut.

It was locked. His den was locked.

"Bonnie?"

"Yes . . ."

Donovan turned. The voice had come from the bedroom. He moved through the open door and saw Bonnie. She was stepping out of the walk-in closet, smoothing her water-stained silk dress. The one she had bought in Paris.

Bonnie's blue eyes widened innocently when she looked up. Her lovely, surgically sculpted features registered a mixture of surprise, mild annoyance and deep concern.

"Donovan—is everything all right?" Her breathless tone suggested he looked strange. Instinctively he glanced at the mirror.

Aside from the fact that his eyes popped and his jaw hung slack like some well-dressed basset hound, he seemed all right.

"Yeah, fine. The production meeting was put off so I thought I'd—" He stopped to give her a suspicious stare. "Who's here?"

He asked the question calmly but Bonnie flinched as if he'd slapped her.

"Here?"

Struggling to remain cool Donovan inhaled

through his nostrils the way his Yoga instructor had taught him.

"Mnn . . . what's . . ." He paused to find the right words. "Whose piece of shit van is that out front?"

She blinked, as if wondering whether she should be offended. "No . . . uh, nothing. Just a guy selling, uh . . . pool cleaner."

"Why'd he lock himself in my den?"

It was a damn good question. Bonnie thought so as well. Her expression of deep, sensitive concern began to sag. And with it, too, her beautifully whittled features seemed to crumble. "Well . . . he . . . uh . . ."

*She never was very creative,* Donavon sighed, waiting patiently.

Bonnie started to say something then slowly exhaled. "Oh God . . ." She gave Donovan a weak smile. "Remember my friend Ollie?"

He dutifully rummaged through his memory.

"Yeah, yeah . . . Ollie, right, of course. Ollie *Olerud,* tall, foolish-looking wanker. Some sort of deadbeat po . . ." He noticed Bonnie violently jerking her head toward the den.

Donovan gaped at the closed door as if trying to grasp her meaning.

". . . Ollie is in there?"

Bonnie's features snapped shut and her familiar expression of weary annoyance returned. "Yes, for Christ's sake, Donovan."

"With the pool cleaner?"

Bonnie glared at him with utter contempt. "Donovan, please. Just Ollie."

The churning in Donovan's belly had swelled to a tsunami but his brain still hadn't caught up. In fact, his brain didn't want to catch up.

"Oh, I see. Well, I'm glad he finally got a job. Always pegged him for a deadbeat."

Donovan gave the closed door an apologetic smile. "Happy to be proved wrong. Selling pool cleaner now, eh? Well . . ." He turned to Bonnie for affirmation. ". . . this would be the neighborhood for it."

For a few moments it was quiet. Donovan's smile curled into a thoughtful pout. "Just door-to-door 'running low on chlorine'? That kind of thing?" he asked the den door.

Receiving no answer he turned back to Bonnie. He could taste an acid bile burning the base of his throat. "Quite a coincidence, what? Him stopping by here and you two knowing each other . . ."

Bonnie looked away. "Donovan, please . . ."

Before he could respond Donovan heard the den door open with a loud *clack*.

Both of them stared as a tall, shambling blond

man sporting a wispy beard and a sheepish expression emerged cautiously into the hall. He peered into the bedroom and waved.

"Heya, Donovan, how ya doin', man?"

Donovan gave him a distracted smile. "Good, Ollie, and yourself?"

"Can't complain, man."

"Excellent. Let's get to it then, shall we?"

Without waiting for an answer Donovan went to his bureau and opened the bottom drawer. "We'll take a couple of vacuum hoses," he said cheerfully, digging through the carefully stacked sweaters. "And we probably need a new filter 'round now—or—wait a minute . . ."

Donovan paused and beamed at his wife. "Darling, do we have a swimming pool?"

There was a long awkward silence before Ollie finally spoke up.

"Okay, man, let's be reasonable about this," he said, nervously stroking his beard. "Okay, so I had relations with your old lady, so we're all a little embarrassed and, what the fuck, man, I know it's a drag and you know a guy's gotta . . ."

Ollie glanced at Bonnie and stepped inside the bedroom. "I mean, these things *happen*."

Donovan slowly stood and held something out to Ollie.

It was a shiny black gun.

Ollie hopped back into the hall. "Hey man, I was just kiddin' about the broa . . . we didn't actually have sex . . ." His voice became hurried and confidential, like a fence selling stolen watches. "I was depressed, ya know. I've, uh . . . I've been impotent, ya know, unable to achieve an erection for about a year and I had to talk to someone about it," he added as if that explained everything. At the same time he kept backing down the hall.

His compulsive beard stroking resembled an obscene form of masturbation. Donovan was both repelled and infuriated that Bonnie would fuck such a loathsome lout.

*In my own bloody bed to boot*, Donovan fumed. His first bullet would go right to the groin. Serve the pathetic bastard bloody well right.

Ollie's voice had gone up an octave and he was shuffling back down the hall in tiny mincing steps. "I mean, a year without an erection. Think about it, man . . . unable to achieve an erection . . ."

Donovan raised the gun and clicked back the hammer.

A loud flash of pain dropped Donovan to his knees. Dazed and disoriented, he tried to focus his blurred vision. Through the painful throbbing in his skull he dimly recognized Bonnie's grimacing face.

She was holding something. Something very

familiar. Donovan looked around. Ollie had disappeared.

Still groggy, he pawed the ground for his gun. "Sodding sods," he babbled angrily, ". . . bloody sodding bleeding bollocks . . ."

"Leave him alone," Bonnie shouted.

Before he could reply another bolt of agony crashed into his skull and he sprawled to the floor. Bonnie's shrill voice drilled into his shattered brain.

"You should've seen this coming, you insensitive shit!"

*Of course, thank you,* Donovan thought, *why didn't I see it? It's all my bloody fucking fault.*

He pushed himself to his feet and stood unsteadily, his eyes fixed on the weapon Bonnie was brandishing. He dimly realized it was a small gold statue. A small human form of indeterminate sex, holding high a sword.

Recognition hit him like ice water. "You vicious bitch!" he croaked, advancing on her. "That's my Daytime Television Lifetime Achievement Award."

Bonnie grabbed the trophy by the base and swung it threateningly.

"You cheesy bastard! Stay back."

Unable to maintain his balance Donovan stumbled closer.

Without hesitation Bonnie brought the trophy

down hard, stabbing him in the thigh with the spiked top. Then she ran out the door.

"Owwww, bloody Christ!" Donovan roared after her. "You whore!"

His leg was throbbing and blood was spreading over his linen trousers. Donovan spotted the trophy on the floor and snatched it up.

The sword was stained oily red. The tsunami in his belly suddenly broke free and propelled him hobbling across the room. He rode the energy like a maddened surfer, flinging open the closet door and wildly burrowing through the junk heaped inside.

"All right then . . ." he rasped, flinging tennis rackets, Rollerblades, golf clubs and hiking shoes aside, ". . . all right, we'll play it that way . . ."

*Knashee! Knasheee!*

Donovan blinked and lifted his head at the sound. The screech came from outside. The driveway.

*Knashee! Knashee!*

It was the horrible wheeze of a rusty engine struggling to turn over.

*The poor pathetic sod's truck won't start,* Donovan realized. *Now I've got the bastard.* His short burst of laughter ended in coughing. With renewed purpose he began pulling down shelves and strewing the contents across the floor.

"You want bloody games?" he ranted, chest heaving. "Good then! We'll do bloody games then!"

Reeling drunkenly, he turned from the closet empty-handed.

*Knashee! Knasheeee!*

The engine's desperate whine was joined by an automobile horn as Donovan limped to another closet and began throwing out tennis balls, gym shorts, sneakers and spiked golf shoes until he finally found it.

"Aha!" he roared. "Bloody *evidence*, you bitch! Explain this away . . ."

Clutching his Polaroid camera aloft Donovan limped frantically to the front window. Along the way he dropped the trophy and scooped up his gun.

*Knasheee! Knashroooom, rooom!*

Ollie's motor finally coughed to life over the car horn's furious blare. Just as Donovan reached the window he heard the metallic wrench of gears and saw the dirty white van lurch backward across his lawn. The van made a hard U, exposing its other side. There, stenciled in large black letters, was the pledge that OLLIE'LL FIX IT.

"Explain this away!" Donovan shouted. He lifted the Polaroid to his eye and snapped. The bright flash sheeted the glass window blinding him.

It also ruined the picture.

"Blast! Blast you!" Donovan cursed through clenched teeth.

He was really riding the tsunami now, hanging ten on a monster wave that was burning like lava. Foaming red flames boiled up around him as he lifted his gun and fired.

The first shot shattered the front window but Donovan was pleased to see a geyser of dirt kick up only a few feet from the van's front tire.

The horn continued blaring as Donovan fired again and again at the wildly skidding van. Suddenly the van was gone and the horn stopped.

A second later a screeching Jaguar peeled out of the now cleared drive. His Jaguar.

"Sodding bitch!" Donovan screamed, vainly pulling the trigger on his empty gun.

Dizziness washed over him and he hopped to the couch. "My Jag," he crooned sadly, tossing the gun aside. He grabbed a decanter of bourbon and sat down heavily, his wounded leg sticking out in front of him.

He took a swig of bourbon and went to work.

Chuckling to himself Donovan took snap after snap of his gashed leg, the photos whirring out of the front of the camera and spewing into his lap.

"Explain this away, you painted harlot!" he muttered with a smug grin. Chortling drunkenly he found another film pack and took a series of shots that featured his blood-stained achievement award. The photos whirred and spewed, whirred and spewed with antic speed.

Still chortling he passed out, the Polaroids scattered over him like holiday decorations on a battered tree.

# CHAPTER
# TWO

The high-pitched whine of Dr. Benway's tooth polisher made most of his patients uncomfortable. But Miles was not like most patients. Relaxed and alert, he sat back in the tilted leather chair with a cell phone pressed against his ear as Dr. Benway worked on his dazzling white teeth.

"It's me, any messages?" Miles said, admiring the view outside the window. ". . . Yeah? Just polishing. What else?"

Lips pulled back and teeth bared for Dr. Benway's buffer, Miles ignored the drill-like whir and focused on the checklist of problems Janice was relaying.

Serenity; that was the key to his fabulous success. His ability to remain centered in the face of chaos, confusion or catastrophe.

"Okay . . . tell Amstedler I'll return in twenty minutes," he said, when Dr. Benway withdrew the buffer. "Have Wrigley look up Oliphant vee Oliphant, Commonwealth of Virginia for its relevance to the Chapman filing—wait—she took the kids to Tahoe?"

*Tahoe?* His mind began racing as the dentist deftly inserted the buffer for a final once-over. *Gotcha,* he thought without elation or regret. *Game, set, and match.*

He checked his smile in the mirror Dr. Benway held up. Nobody knew it yet but he was about to break another big case.

Miles loved his work.

He regarded his profession as a calling, like the priesthood or hang gliding. And in a few short years he had floated to the crest of the mountain. From California to New York the rich and the would-be rich uttered his name in hushed tones.

Miles Massey—the Terminator—hands down the best damn divorce attorney in Hollywood.

Serenity; that was the secret. Of course, the Percodan did help.

Later, while driving his Mercedes into the bright blue California sky, Miles called Janice on the hands-free phone, which allowed him to concentrate on traffic while he outlined his brilliant game plan. From time to time he glimpsed other drivers alone in their cars, talking or singing into the empty air.

"Which side of Tahoe?" he asked carefully. "Great! If the cruise goes all the way around the lake she left the state and she's in breach. Tell Wrigley to prepare a filing to attach."

He grinned into the rearview mirror. His perfect teeth gleamed back. "Everything, of course. Primary residence, beach house, ski cabin, stocks, bonds, dental floss . . ."

He absently changed lanes and noticed a young blonde surfer girl in the next car. She smiled and cocked her head as if telling him to follow. A moment later the sunlight blinked off as the Mercedes slipped into a fluorescent tunnel.

"Gonna lose you," he called.

He glanced over at the next lane but the blonde was gone.

Janice was in love with her boss.

She felt privileged to work with Miles Massey. He depended on her and she was there for him day in and day out. Just the way she wanted it.

She felt a pang of disappointment when the phone chirped off. While waiting for him to call back she made careful notes of their conversation. Crisp and efficient—that was her forte. Which was why she made the big bucks and was roundly envied by the other girls in the firm.

With his suave good looks and smoldering dark eyes Miles was a combination of Cary Grant and Elvis. Every female he met crumbled when he flashed his nuclear smile.

However he seemed oblivious, too immersed in his work to find time for romance. Oh, there were women, of course, but nothing serious. Janice wondered if his constant encounters with unhappy couples had made him gun-shy.

She adjusted her head set and fantasized about having sex with Miles. . . . She is lying on a couch in candlelit room; Miles, in a silk dressing gown, fills her glass with champagne. He leans closer and kisses her. . . .

His voice broke through her reverie. "You there?"

"Uh-huh," she said huskily.

"Tell Fred Armatrading that we finally have pictures of his wife with the tennis pro. Oh! And we'll need a fruit and pastry basket for my nine-thirty in the conference room. I didn't have time for breakfast this morning."

*Where were you last night,* Janice thought, but there was no trace of curiosity or reproach in her tone. "Fruit and pastry, conference room."

A familiar prickle across her skin alerted her.

"Where are you?" Janice asked, looking around.

The phone clicked off.

"Comin' right atcha," Miles announced cheerfully, striding through the front door. "What's up?"

Janice smothered her fluttering heart and coolly checked her schedule. "Your nine o'clock is here. Bonnie Donnelly."

Miles scooped up her compact and checked his teeth in the mirror.

"Bonnie Donnelly," he repeated. It sounded like a war cry.

Janice watched adoringly as Miles straightened his tie and marched into his office, armed with his briefcase and that hundred-megaton smile.

"Mrs. Donnelly!" she heard him trumpet, before he shut the door.

Bonnie Donnelly had all the classic elements of a Beverly Hills matron: body by Jake, hair by José, face by Monsanto. Miles had seen a thousand like her and he had ushered them all to the promised land.

Even now, faced with irrefutable evidence of Bonnie's transgressions, Miles was serenely confident of victory. He shuffled the stack of Polaroids like a tarot deck and dealt them onto his desk one by one.

"Mnn, yes . . ." He peered at the photos as if trying to read the future. "Your husband showed remarkable foresight in taking these pictures," he conceded. "And yes, in the absence of a swimming pool the presence of a pool man would appear to be suspicious."

Miles leaned back in his leather chair, fingers steepled thoughtfully. "But madam, who is the real victim here? Let me suggest the following. Your husband, who on a prior occasion had slapped you—*beat* you, I think that word is not inappropriate . . ."

Bonnie seemed confused. "But I . . ."

"Let me finish, please," Miles said gently. "I'm not interested in who slapped whom first. Your husband, who has beaten you—repeatedly."

"He . . ."

Miles held up his hand. "Please—repeatedly, was at the time brandishing your firearm—"

"It's *his* gun."

"And we'll get it back for you," Miles assured. "Brandishing a firearm, trying in his rage to shoot an acquaintance—a friend of long standing."

"They never really cared for each other."

Miles waved the comment aside. "So he says now—an old friend, *and* but for your cool intervention, his tantrum might have ended this shmoe's life—and ruined his own."

He leaned forward and lowered his voice. "As for the sexual indiscretion which he imagined had taken place, wasn't it in fact *he* who has been sleeping with the pool man?"

Bonnie stared at him in stunned disbelief.

Miles stood up and began to pace around his lavishly appointed office.

"No? Am I going too far here?" He paused to study her. "Were his sexual, uh . . ."

"Mr. Massey," she said indignantly.

Miles threw up his hands in surrender. "Okay. I'm not omniscient. But my point is that he acted upon an assumption which he cannot prove and which you, I take it, totally deny."

Bonnie's expression wavered. "Well . . ."

"Fine," Miles congratulated. "That's all I needed to know. I'll take this case. But . . ." He lifted a warning finger. ". . . it is *imperative* that I discuss matters with Oliver Olerud before we proceed any further. To work out the kinks, so to speak, in our testimony."

For the first time Bonnie saw a ray of hope.

Ever since she opened the "gift package" Donovan had sent to her hotel bungalow, Bonnie had resigned herself to life in the slow lane. The pictures he sent were hard evidence of her attack on her husband. There was also one shot of Ollie's van cutting across the lawn. Despite the bad lighting, Ollie's business logo was clearly visible on the van's side. Adultery and assault—a deadly combo in a divorce proceeding. She'd be lucky to get minimum wage.

Or so she believed before meeting Miles Massey.

The ray of hope she glimpsed expanded, filling the plush office with a golden light that shimmered around the handsome lawyer like a halo. Miles Massey was her shining knight, her champion.

Business aside, she was also intensely aware of the lawyer's physical charms. Savage, sensual and sensitive; a three-way Bonnie found impossible to resist.

"You really think we can put all this across?" she asked breathlessly.

Miles perched on the corner of his desk and gave a light, burbling laugh. To Bonnie it sounded like Mozart.

"The truth of the matter is so self-evident to me," he declared, "that I'm sure I can make it quite transparent to a jury—should your husband choose to push it that far."

His tone implied Donovan would be foolish to try. Bonnie discreetly tugged her skirt an inch or two higher.

Miles glanced at his watch, signaling the end of the meeting. He got to his feet.

"We'll need to caucus again to try to draw up a picture of your husband's net worth," he told her briskly. "A map of enemy territory, so to speak. You said he's a TV producer."

"He has a soap opera, *The Sands of Time*. It's a silly show," she added, giddy with her new sense of power.

"Well, it'll be yours soon," he said soothingly.

He took her arm and for a wild moment Bonnie thought he was going to kiss her. Instead he escorted her across the room and opened the door.

Still hoping, Bonnie turned and looked deep into his dark eyes. "Thank you, Mr. Massey," she whispered.

He gave her a modest wave and shut the door.

Miles ambled back to his chair and leaned back. For a few long minutes he gazed out the window at the Hollywood Hills.

"Still," he murmured with a wistful smile, "you have to admire him for taking those pictures."

# CHAPTER
# THREE

Wrigley was worried.

In all the time he had served as Miles Massey's junior associate he'd never seen the celebrated attorney act so strangely. Strange *wasn't the word for it,* Wrigley reflected glumly. *Suicidal* would be more accurate.

The way Miles was comporting himself during this trial was sheer professional suicide. He was allowing the opposing attorney total leeway. In fact, he wasn't even listening to the testimony. Miles kept fidgeting like a schoolboy and looking out the window while Freddy Bender questioned his client Mrs. Guttman. Or rather, while Bender guided Mrs. Guttman through his prepared script.

"Mrs. Guttman, you have testified that you

were your husband's sexual slave for thirty-six years. Ever since you were married."

Mrs. Guttman patted her silver bouffant. "Except for two years when he was in the navy, in Southeast Asia."

Wrigley waited for Miles to object but he was busy drawing a picture of the judge.

"What's wrong with you today?" Wrigley hissed.

Miles didn't look up. "I'm bored."

"Prior to your marriage, what was your profession?" Bender asked innocently.

Wrigley knew better. It was the hook, to prove that she had been plucked from a well-paying profession which she was now unable to continue. Miles knew better, too, but he just sat there, chin in hand.

"I was a hostess for Braniff Airlines," Mrs. Guttman answered.

"You can't be bored," Wrigley whispered. "It's unprofessional."

Miles shrugged. "I can't help it. You don't *decide* to become bored. It happens."

Meanwhle Bender was moving in for the kill. "And what is your husband's profession?"

"He manufactures staples and industrial Bradtacks," Mrs. Guttman recited dutifully. "He's very successful."

"You're just looking for trouble," Wrigley

muttered. "It's a midlife crisis. Look, get yourself a new car."

Miles kept drawing. "I have a new car. I have two new cars. I'm on the tab at the Mercedes dealership."

"Couldn't you just have walked away from this abusive relationship?" Bender wondered, face turned toward the jury.

It was a question Miles should be asking, Wrigley noted.

To his dismay, Miles was still wrestling with his angst. "I've torn down the house twice and just redid the cabin in Vail," he confided with a weary sigh. "I've got three gardeners, a cook and a guy who waxes my jet."

"No. I couldn't just walk out." Mrs. Guttman sniffled and took a lace hanky from her sleeve. "He had the videos."

Wiping her eyes Mrs. Guttman drew herself up for the climax to her performance. "He would invite these girls home from the staple factory, to our condo in Palm Springs."

Miles just kept rambling on. "My accountant keeps asking me why I still go in to work. Goddammit, I need a challenge. This . . ." He waved dismissively at the courtroom. ". . . is not a challenge. I need something I can sink my teeth into, professionally speaking."

"He had a device he called the Intruder," Mrs. Guttman told the world.

"The problem is that everyone is willing to compromise," Miles went on. "That's the problem with the institution of marriage. It's *based* on compromise. Even through it's dissolution." He gestured at the well-coiffed female in the witness stand. "Mrs. Guttman here is going to score some points concerning her husband's sexual politics. Naturally we'll try to impeach. The process will find an equilibrium point determined by the skill of the opposing lawyers, and then each party will walk away with a portion of the staple factory."

Freddy Bender looked shocked. "The Intruder, you say?"

Wrigley's boyish features showed signs of irritation. "That's just life, Miles. Life is compromise . . ."

"No, Wrigley, that is *death*. Challenge, struggle and of course the ultimate destruction of your opponent—that's life. Let me ask you something. Ivan the Terrible, Henry the Eighth and Attila the Hun; what did they have in common?"

Wrigley thoughtfully removed his glasses and peered at Miles.

"Middle names?"

Miles looked up. His zealous intensity and

hoarse voice gave him the aspect of a wild-eyed missionary. "These men didn't *just* win. These men . . ."

"Mr. Massey!"

Startled, Wrigley glanced around. Everyone was staring at them; the spectators, jury, Freddy Bender, Mrs. Guttman and especially Judge Boone.

"Mr. Massey," Boone said acidly, gavel poised in midair as if about to pronounce a death sentence. "I ask again if you have any questions for the complainant?"

Wrigley felt his face flush red under Boone's withering glare. Miles, on the other hand, was the paradigm of composure. His messianic fervor was smoothly leavened by an apologetic smile.

"I'm sorry, Your Honor," Miles said earnestly. "I was just consulting with my associate."

Technically true, Wrigley noted. They just weren't consulting about the case. With grudging admiration he watched Miles rise and casually approach the sobbing Mrs. Guttman. It was the moment they had been waiting for. Wrigley felt his belly churn.

"Now then, Mrs. Guttman," Miles said gently. He paused and looked at the jury. "Could you tell us who David Gonzales is?"

Mrs. Guttman stopped sniffling and blinked at him apprehensively.

"Well . . ." she puckered her collagen lips as if trying to remember. "He's the tennis pro . . . at the club."

Miles sadly shook his head. "Ah ha . . ."

Both Mrs. Guttman and Freddy Bender stiffened as Miles reached back and Wrigley put a sheaf of papers in his hand. For a millimoment, Wrigley felt as if he'd passed the sword to the matador. It was glorious.

"He's the tennis pro at the club," Miles said, voice steely cold as he lifted the papers. "Then why are your letters to him addressed 'Dear David and Goliath'?"

*Two ears and a tail,* Wrigley exulted in watching Freddy Bender vainly plead with the judge. He was in the presence of greatness.

Miles took it all in stride. He packed up his briefcase, gave the jury a brilliant smile and was off to the next battle.

Attilla the Hun would have been proud.

# CHAPTER
# FOUR

Rex Rexroth was a great fan of American history. He especially liked the period when the West expanded with the railroad. Someday he intended to produce an epic movie about the rail splitters and gandy dancers who laid steel tracks across the wild frontier. Those brawny heroes with iron hammers—and the women who followed them.

Women like the one beside him in his Mercedes rocking a champagne bottle like a baby against her ample breasts. As Nina moved her body in time to "Poppa Was a Rolling Stone" Rex could imagine her as a dance hall whore in some rough frontier town.

Rex was rich, but not rich enough to finance a

hundred-million-dollar production. No, that would come later, after he put this deal across. Meanwhile he needed to relax. And Nina knew how to party.

Rex checked his rearview and saw nothing but distant headlights. He had a sense of being followed all day but it was probably just adrenaline. He'd been looking forward to this all week.

Rex loved to cheat on his wife. Granted, Marilyn was an exquisite beauty but domestic bliss seemed to dampen his lust. Anyway, Marilyn didn't connect with his darker side, Rex observed, swinging the car into the motor court. Not like Nina, bless her wicked heart.

Nina staggered out, still swaying to the music. Rex glanced around and exited the Mercedes. After checking the area a second time, Rex tried to straighten his bow tie then saw his shirt and tuxedo jacket were smudged with Nina's lipstick. He would have to buy a new tux tomorrow. No sense inciting Marilyn. She was such a trusting angel.

He threw an arm around Nina's creamy shoulders and guided her, giggling, to one of the cabins.

Neither of them noticed the Infiniti stopped outside the motor court, just under the sign that read MALIBU CABINS BY THE SEA. They weren't supposed to notice, Gus reflected smugly, watching them reel across the lot. That was the whole damn point.

As soon as they entered the cabin Rex locked the door. When he turned around Nina had disappeared but her evening gown was tossed on the bed.

*Showtime!*

Rex put an imaginary train whistle to his lips. *"Chooo, chooo!"*

Loosening his tie he began searching the cabin; under the bed, inside the closet. Then he heard a voice coming from the far wall.

*"Chugga, chugga—chugga, chugga . . ."* Nina sang huskily.

It was the mating cry Rex had been dreaming about. He felt himself getting hard and hurridly threw off his jacket. *"Ch, ch—ch, ch . . ."*

*"Chugga, chugga-chugga, chugga . . ."*

Rex saw a long leg emerge from behind the window curtain. A salacious smile spread across his face. *"Ch, ch—ch, ch,"* he hissed in panting counterpoint to Nina's husky *chuggas.*

When he drew the curtain aside Nina was standing there in red panties and bra, with a conductor's cap perched saucily on her head. Rex again lifted his imaginary whistle.

"*Choo! Choo!*"

He began stripping off his clothes, Nina helping him.

"*Chugga, chugga—chugga, chugga . . .*" She continued breathlessly pulling off his trousers. She paused to admire his erection.

"Pull your ears in, Rexie, you're comin' to a tunnel!" Nina called, unhooking her bra.

"*Choo, choo . . .*" Rex lunged at Nina and wrestled her onto the bed.

But as soon as the train entered the station the engine blew up. The door slammed open with a loud crash. A stocky black man with a video camera glued to his face and a porkpie hat on his head rushed into the room.

Nina screamed and scrambled behind the curtain as Rex leaped from the bed. They were both too late.

"I'm gonna nail your ass!" the man cried, panning from Nina to Rex.

Rex darted from side to side, trying to retrieve his clothes off-camera but the black man was relentless.

"I'm gonna nail your ass!" he repeated, cornering Rex, who was trying to put on his trousers. Rex bent over, mooning the camera as he tried to get dressed and out of there. Nina kept screeching but the man's voice was louder.

"I'm gonna nail your ass!"

To Rex it sounded like the mantra from hell. And he was right.

Gus Fetch slipped the cassette into the VCR and strolled back to the couch. He was quite aware of Marilyn Rexroth's anticipation—and distaste. They were all that way the first time. As for him, it was his favorite part of the job. The world premiere of another Gus Fetch surveillance video.

Marilyn Rexroth watched grimly as her husband looked up from his sexual cavorting and gaped at the camera in disbelief before jumping out of the frame.

"I nailed his ass," Gus told her.

Marilyn kept her attention on the screen. "Trains . . ." she murmered.

Gus squinted at her. Marilyn Rexroth was beautiful—and classy. Classy was a rare commodity lately, he reflected. She was a cool brunette with a pedigree, well spoken, elegant and sensual at the same time. A diamond as big as a pomegranate was mounted on a ring on her left hand.

". . . I thought he'd outgrown trains," she said, still watching the TV.

Gus snorted. "They never grow up, lady. They just get tubby."

"How charming." She gave him an icy glance. "And appropriate."

Gus shifted uncomfortably. Normally the wronged wife would be shocked, distraught and vulnerable. But this babe had it together. "Yeah," he said casually, "I've always had ample proportions. But it's all muscle—I'm as hard as a rock," he added suggestively but drew no reaction. "I'm not one of these cream puff, sit-behind-a-desk private dicks. I'm an ass nailer."

Marilyn smiled. "So I see."

Faintly Gus heard himself shouting *I'm gonna nail your ass* as Rex Rexroth hopped around in the foreground. Inspired, he drifted back to his favorite topic, himself. "Gym four times a week, an hour and a half plus stretching, Lifecycle, Lifestep, LifeCircuit . . . Gus Fetch doesn't fuck around."

She shot him another nasty glance, even colder than the last.

"I must say, you don't exhibit a great deal of tact for someone in your line of work."

Gus shrugged. "Look, lady, you want tact, call a tactician. You want an ass nailed, call Gus Fetch. Cripes, you look as if you're takin' it pretty good," he added, a shrewd smile on his bulldog face. "I seen 'em carry on like Baptists at a funeral. Like they hired me to prove their husbands *wasn't* foolin' around."

Her expression softened a notch. "Oh, don't misunderstand, Mr., uh . . ."

"Fetch, Gus Fetch."

"While I don't find it terribly amusing, I am grateful that you got this, uh, material. Grateful and delighted." She gazed at the monitor, chin high and eyes shining like Joan of Arc in the middle of the bonfire.

"This is going to be my passport to wealth, independence, freedom . . ." she whispered, almost to herself.

Gus yawned. "Sounds to me like you're gonna nail his ass."

# CHAPTER
# FIVE

Marilyn wasn't overly shocked by her husband's infidelity.

It was a key factor in her master plan. She knew quite well she had married an indiscreet fool. In fact she was counting on Rex to do something impulsive and stupid. But this railroad thing . . .

Marilyn shuddered and slipped a CD into the player. The lyric strains of Vivaldi lifted her spirits. Rex had tried to entice her into his choo-choo train fetish but Marilyn found it weird, infantile and not very sexy. It was also silly.

His sleazy stoker seemed to enjoy it well enough, she observed. Even though this was exactly what she wanted, Marilyn felt a twinge of jealousy.

Lost in *The Four Seasons* she drifted from room to room taking inventory. Perhaps she wouldn't sell it for a while, Marilyn speculated. She liked living in Malibu.

She caught a glimpse of herself in the gilded mirror and moved nearer. She liked what she saw. Her face and body were real, untouched by plastic surgery. Maybe she was a tad fuller that the hard bodies that abounded in Malibu, but that's the way a real woman should look. A real woman. Not a squeaky little girl with implants.

Unfortunately her husband, Rex, never figured out the difference. Too bad, Marilyn reflected. He could have gotten so much more for his money.

A persistent scratching sound at the front door drew her attention. Marilyn remained calm. She knew what it was. Her husband was trying to get into her house.

Pausing at the mirror to fix her hair, Marilyn went to the front door. Sure enough, she could see Rex from the side window. He was bent over the doorknob with a look of pure hatred. He produced another key and when that didn't work, he furiously rattled the knob. Finally he had the wit to try the bell.

Marilyn heard the distant sound of chimes

and Rex's voice behind the door. "Honey? . . . honey?"

*Honey,* she thought disdainfully. How common, how unimaginative, how fucking unromantic. Disgusted, she pressed the intercom button.

"Rex, get away from the door."

"Honey, my key doesn't work. Can we talk about this?"

"Rex, get away from the door."

"Honey, I know you're upset . . ."

With each *honey,* Marilyn's fury escalated. How could this banal buffoon have the balls to cheat on her? It was insufferable, she told herself.

"Rex, get away from the door. I don't like having to set the dogs on you."

He ignored the warning. "Oh, for crying out loud. Just hear me out for one min—*dogs?*"

Rex jerked back from the door but it was too late. A large, slavering rottweiler was bounding around the corner of the house. He turned and ran but a second rottweiler scrambled across the lawn after him.

Rex sprinted for his car, the dogs snarling and biting at his heels. Gasping for breath, he mustered a desperate effort and lunged inside his Mercedes just ahead of the ravening beasts. Undaunted, the dogs feverishly pushed their snouts into the half-open window. Rex threw himself across the leather seats and fumbled with the window buttons. In panic he pressed down and the window began to open farther. Growling and foaming, the dogs strained to push inside until he found the right button and the windows rolled up, squeezing them out like toothpaste.

Rex heard his heart drumming rapidly above the rottweilers' barking as they lunged repeatedly at the window. Wishing he still smoked, he took a few deep breaths, then picked up the car phone and punched in a number.

As it rang, Rex leaned back and wistfully gazed at the stately white Spanish-style hacienda, his emotions reeling from disbelief to depression. *This can't be happening*, he told himself.

But the snarling beasts scratching at his door told him he was fucked.

He was still gazing at the house when Marilyn coolly answered from within. ". . . Yes, dogs. I wanted some security since I'll be living here alone."

*Alone*. The word confirmed his deepest, darkest fear. *But Marilyn is so sweet, so trusting*, Rex thought frantically. He made a great effort to stay calm.

He lowered his voice, trying to sound soothing and apologetic at the same time. "But honey, you know a divorce would ruin me right now.

Everything I have—everything we have—is tied up in my business."

"Then you'll just have to sell your business, won't you, dear?"

Rex felt a vise twist around his belly. One dog kept scratching at the window while the other leaped on the hood and was snarling down at him.

"The business is my entire life!" he pleaded, half sobbing.

"Your entire life, Rex?" Her voice came down like a sword. "Aren't you forgetting the Atcheson, Topeka, and the Santa Fe?"

"Cheap shot, Marilyn. You know that's just a . . . hobby."

"And an expensive one. Good-bye, Rex."

"Honey? . . . honey? . . . what, what the—" The dog on the hood had stopped barking and was oddly hunched over, shivering slightly.

"Oh my God, no . . ." Rex groaned as he watched the dog drop a thick pile of steaming shit on the hood of his Mercedes.

He grabbed the phone and hurridly punched another number. He needed serious help. He needed the Terminator.

Miles was still bored.

It was all he could do to listen to the information Janice was rapidly spewing at him as he strode purposefully down the central corridor of Massey, Myerson. Janice stayed right behind him, referring to a small spiral notebook.

"You have a discovery hearing at five-thirty for the Maxine Gopnik case."

"Discovery for the Gopnik . . ." Miles said absently.

"And a Lance Kelso called—he read your article about palimony settlements in same-sex partnerships and would like to schedule an appointment."

"Same-sex Kelso . . ." Miles droned, marching ahead.

"Arthur Yardumian and his tax attorney want to reschedule their caucus for tomorrow. Arthur had to fly to Atlanta for a deadbeat dad hearing."

"Yardumian in Atlanta . . ." Although his mind was elsewhere he automatically stored there information for future retrieval like some robot computer. *The R2D2 of divorce,* Miles thought unhappily. He yearned for some human connection, a challenge or mission. He yearned for . . .

He didn't know. *That's the problem when you have everything,* Miles brooded.

Janice kept giving him information in her usual crisp, efficient manner. "And your ten-thirty is here—Rex Rexroth."

The name evoked a glimmer of interest. Miles stopped and gave her an inquisitive look.

His intense expression never failed to melt her heart, as well as various other body parts, but Janice maintained her cool. She rubbed her fingers against her thumb, making the universal money sign.

"Real estate," Janice confided, "he's okay."

Miles threw his shoulders back and headed for his office. "Rex Rexroth . . ." he murmered. To Janice it sounded like a call to arms.

Miles Massey's office had been featured three times in *World of Interiors* magazine and each time the décor was different.

This season it was done in 1930s Deco straight out of a Fred Astaire movie, with a rounded white bar, white leather stools, chrome and glass tables, sculptures by Erté and etchings by Icart. An erotic black-and-white drawing by Tom Ungerer was discreetly hung in the corner behind the bar.

Rex was admiring the drawing when Miles entered.

"Mr. Rexroth."

He waved off the formality. "Rex, please."

"Miles Massey." He flashed a brilliant smile. "Please sit, relax and consider this office *your*

office, your haven, your war room, for the dura-
tion of our campaign."

He has style, Rex conceded. This was going to
cost him. "Thank you," he sighed, easing wearily
into a black leather chair. The bed at the motel
sagged and Nina snored.

Miles sat in the black executive chair behind
his white desk, leaned back, made a steeple with
his fingers and assumed an expression of deepest gravitas.

"Tell me your troubles."

Rex snorted and laughed ruefully, a bit nervous. It was almost like going to a shrink, or a
hooker for the first time. "Jeez . . . where do I
start?"

Miles gave him a manly smile of encourage-
ment.

"Well, my wife has me between a rock and a
hard place."

"That's her job," Miles said serenely. "You
have to respect that."

Rex shook his head. "When I first met
Marilyn . . . well, we were crazy about each other.
Not emotionally, of course," he added, recalling
her refusal to play night train. "We just couldn't
keep our hands off each other."

Miles validated their passion with a somber
nod. "Mnn."

"But then . . . but then . . ." Rex's voice trailed sadly off.

"Time marches on . . . ardor cools," Miles intoned, as if delivering a eulogy.

Rex tried to toughen up and get to the point—his money.

"Yeah. So, uh . . . well, we had an understanding."

"Whereby . . . ?"

"We could see other people. You know—see them."

"And was this understanding documented in any way?"

Rex shifted nervously. "No, it was just . . . understood."

"I understand." Miles sat upright. "Let me ask you this then, friend Rex. Has Mrs. Rexroth pursued the . . . opportunities implicit in your arrangement?"

"I . . . I can only assume . . ."

"Not in court you can't," Miles said flatly. He drummed his fingers on the desk. "Has she retained counsel?"

"I'm not sure. She has rottweilers."

"Not a good sign. And have you yourself exploited your . . . understood freedom?"

"There's a young lady," Rex admitted sheepishly. "She . . . she lets me be myself."

Miles absolved him with a shrug. "Of course. And your wife is aware and/or has evidence?"

"Video."

The word hung in the air like a noose.

"Mnnn . . ." Miles folded his arms. "And to cut to the chase, forensically speaking, is there a prenup?"

Rex's gave the helpless sigh of a man pleading guilty to his own murder.

Miles sighed sympathetically. "The fault, dear Brutus, is not in the stars but in ourselves," he quoted.

Again, Rex felt he was at a funeral.

"Well, let me ask you this: What kind of settlement do you seek? What are, for you, the parameters of the possible?"

"Well, you see that's the problem." Rex sat up and looked Miles Massey directly in the eye. "I can't afford to give her anything."

"Nothing?"

"I know it sounds rough but I'm about to close a deal to develop some mini-malls, and I'm mortgaged up to my heinie. If this deal goes south I'm ruined—I'll lose millions . . ." His voice cracked and he looked away.

# CHAPTER
## SIX

The Malibu Club served as social center for trophy wives who wanted to stay in shape and shop around for a young lover. Sarah Sorkin, Ramona Barcelona and Claire O'Mara were regulars, meeting there almost every afternoon to gossip and complain about their rich husbands.

At the moment they were ensconced on a couch consulting their Filofaxes as health club disco throbbed over the public address.

Sarah looked up. She was tightly built and had a tendency to wag her blonde head when she spoke. "Why don't you all come out to see my beach house tomorrow?" she chirped brightly.

Ramona couldn't stand her cheerleader act.

She rolled her lustrous black eyes but didn't look up. "I didn't know Dimitri had a beach house."

"Neither did I until my lawyer found it," Sarah said smugly. "It was quite a paper trail. Dimitri had it in the dog's name."

Ramona gave her an *aren't men disgusting?* shrug. "Mnn, yeah—well, tomorrow won't work. I'm having a body wrap. How's Wednesday?"

*She'd have to wrap an entire rain forest around her body to lose that flab,* Sarah thought. She smiled sweetly. "Wednesday? Hair appointment in the morning. Afternoon?"

"Shrink." Ramona ran a long purple finger-nail down the page. "How's your Thursday?"

"I'm having facial injections. That kills Friday and Saturday."

"Botox?" Claire asked, suddenly interested.

"Butt fat."

Ramona looked up. "Does that really work?"

Sarah struck a pose. "You tell me."

Ramona maintained a frozen smile as she inspected Sarah's seamless face. Botox or butt fat, she looked like a wax dummy. Fortunately Ramona was spared by Marilyn's appearance.

All three women watched Marilyn Rexroth breeze across the lobby with all the envy due a smashing beauty. Her long legs and lush hips swayed in sensual rhythm as she walked, as graceful in high heels as she was barefoot. Unlike the other girls, she actually read books and her intelligence enhanced her flawless features.

Marilyn blew air kisses all around and settled into an easy chair.

"Hello, darlings."

Ramona didn't bother with small talk. She blurted the question they were all dying to ask. "So you and Rex are . . ."

Marilyn smiled impishly. "Mnn, yes. As my private detective puts it, 'we're going to nail his ass.' "

"I've been trying to nail George's ass for years," Ramona declared. "But he's so fucking *careful*."

Claire began to cough, spitting up some of her Gatorade.

"Are you all right, Claire?" Marilyn cooed. Everyone knew about George and Claire except Ramona.

"Down the wrong pipe," Claire said hastily. "Who's your lawyer?"

"Freddie Bender. We've got a meeting this afternoon with Rex and his schnauzer."

"Good choice," Sarah said. "Who's Rex's guy?"

"Miles Massey."

The name triggered an instant reaction. All three women gasped and stared wide-eyed at Marilyn as if she had invoked Satan himself.

"Miles Massey of Massey, Myerson?" Ramona said in a hushed voice.

A shadow of concern crossed Marilyn's face. "Do you know him?"

"By reputation." Ramona leaned closer. Sarah and Claire leaned with her. "And he's no schnauzer. He got Anne Rumsey that cute little island of George's!"

Sarah nodded solemnly. "George was so impressed, he hired him when he divorced his second."

"Muriel Rumsey," Claire said, shaking her head.

Marilyn smiled. "Who's she?"

"Now?" Sarah lowered her voice. "She's a night manager at McDonald's."

"They call him the Terminator," Claire whispered.

Marilyn's smile faded. Then she remembered the video.

Not even this legal Lucifer could deny the glaring evidence of Rex and Nina naked on camera, she assured herself. Anyway, Massey was just a man and that was something she could handle.

"But Marilyn, do we have a man for you!" Ramona declared as if reading her mind. "He just separated from his third."

"Thorstenson Gieselensen!" Sarah said brightly. "He's in fish."

"He *is* fish," Ramona corrected.

Sarah wrinkled her new nose. "Well, he's tuna."

"*She's* keeping his name," Claire said.

"And one of his planes," Sarah added smugly.

Ramona clasped her hands to her bosom. "And all seven children."

"And only two are hers." Sarah gave Marilyn a knowing smile. "Massey."

Again, the dread name dampened their enthusiasm.

"But he's still tuna," Ramona reminded.

All three women nodded wisely. Marilyn gave them a grateful smile but she wasn't in the mood. If Massey was that tough she needed to be on top of her game—and without reproach.

"Please, ladies," she said with all the dignity she could muster. "I'm not seeing anyone until I finish nailing Rex's ass."

Sarah looked shocked. "But Marilyn! This is tuna!"

Marilyn managed a Madonna smile that suggested years of self-denial. "One husband at a time."

The Miles Massey conference room was designed to intimidate.

The plush executive chairs afforded clients and adversaries a stunning view of the hills through floor-to-ceiling windows. In front of each chair, built into the black mahogany conference table, was a computer port. At the moment, a large basket of fruit and pastries stood in the center of the table.

Miles nibbled thoughtfully on a strawberry as he mentally prepared himself for the meeting.

Although merely a primary encounter, a formality, this meeting was crucial, Miles reflected. Like Sumo wrestling or street fighting, the first move determined the outcome.

Rex watched his attorney with a queasy smile. He hadn't seen Marilyn since she booted him out and he was nervous. Excited, too.

The buzzer broke the silence. The enemy had arrived.

"I'll do the talking," Miles said, making sure Rex understood. "I know you'll be tempted to chime in but—remember—you are in an emotionally vulnerable state. I'm a professional."

"Oh, okay," Rex said, eyes on the door.

The majestic double doors swung open and Marilyn strode inside wearing a black silk Jil Sanders suit that caressed her regal form. Freddy Bender was a step behind, consort and consigliere to the queen warrior.

Rex almost fainted but Miles casually rose to greet them.

Miles purposely ignored Marilyn Rexroth. "Freddy," he said warmly, shaking the attorney's hand. "Good to see you again."

"This is Rex," Miles announced, ushering Freddy to the table. He looked back as if noticing Marilyn Rexroth for the first time.

"And you must be the lovely Marilyn."

She gave him an icy smile. "Mrs. Rexroth, please. And you must be Mr. Massey."

Miles bowed slightly. "Miles, please."

He *is* good, Marilyn conceded as they settled around the table. She was well aware of Mr. Massey's little mind games. She had played enough of them herself. But she was pleased to see that her attorney was having none of it.

Freddy kept his arms folded and his face grim as he waited for Miles to speak.

"So, Freddy," Miles said, offering him the food basket, "I was sorry to hear about the Goldberger Award. Pastry?"

Nicely done, Marilyn noted. No one mentioned he was drop-dead handsome.

Freddy Bender glared at Miles. The Goldberger thing was a low blow. "We did very well," he said curtly.

Miles gave Marilyn an innocent smile. "Ha,

ha. Don't worry, Mrs. Rexroth, you're ably represented. I'm sure Freddy's too modest to have told you he used to clerk for Clarence Thomas. Pastry? It's going begging."

"Don't try to bait me, Miles," Freddy warned. "If you've got a proposal to make, let's hear it."

"Well, at this point," Miles paused and gazed fondly at Rex, "my client is prepared to consider reconciliation."

Marilyn avoided Rex's pleading eyes. She was much more interested in the debonair attorney pleading her husband's case.

Freddy waved off the suggestion like an annoying fly. "My client has ruled that out."

Rex sighed loudly. Everyone pretended not to hear.

Miles scooped up a clipboard and tapped it with his Mont Blanc pen.

"My client is prepared to entertain an amicable dissolution of their marriage without prejudice."

Freddy snorted. "That's a fart in a stiff wind."

Miles calmly moved on. "My client proposes a thirty-day cooling-off period."

"My client feels sufficiently dispassionate," Freddy droned. He knew the routine.

Miles countered. "My client asks that you not initiate proceedings pending his settling certain affairs in order."

Freddy looked at Miles. "Ha, ha, ha," he laughed as if finally getting the joke.

Marilyn couldn't help laughing along with him. Here was her errant husband, caught in flagrant adultery, asking her to wait in virtual poverty while he made a huge profit on her money.

Miles gave her a sheepish, kid-in-the-cookie-jar smile. "Heh, heh."

Rex glared at them suspiciously. "What's so goddamned funny?"

Miles laid an assuring hand on his arm. "Please, Rex—let me handle this." He tossed the clipboard aside and carefully studied Bender.

"All right, so much for icebreakers," Miles said evenly. He poured a glass of water. "What're you after, Freddy?"

"My client is prepared to settle for fifty percent of the marital assets."

Miles choked, spraying water. "Why only fifty percent, Freddy? Why not ask for a hundred percent? As long as we're dreaming, why not a hundred and fifty?" He leaned back in his chair. "Are you familiar with Kershner?" He made it sound like nerve gas.

Freddy was unfazed. "Kershner does not apply."

"Just bring this to trial and we'll see if Kershner applies."

The two men locked eyes. Marilyn watched in fascination. She knew Miles was her foe but his little boy smile had gotten to her.

"What's Kershner?" Rex asked.

Miles kept his eyes on Freddy. "Please—let me handle this."

"Kershner was in Kentucky," Freddy said.

Miles looked skeptical. "Kershner was in Kentucky?"

"Kershner was in Kentucky," Freddy said flatly.

Miles shrugged. "Okay, Freddy, let's forget Kershner—what's your bottom line?"

"The primary residence plus thirty percent of the remaining assets."

Miles grinned in disbelief. "Are you kidding? Have you forgotten Kershner?"

Freddy's face reddened. He stood up and angrily shut his attaché case. Miles looked at him with innocent surprise.

"Freddy, it's a negotiation, we're all friends here."

"I'll see you at the preliminary," Freddy said, heading for the door.

Miles plucked a croissant from the basket. "Fine," he called to Freddy's retreating back. "*We'll* eat the pastry."

Freddy kept walking, but just as Marilyn reached the door, she couldn't resist glancing back. Miles Massey was a most disturbing man. She didn't know whether to fear him or seduce him.

# CHAPTER
# SEVEN

When he wasn't busy nailing asses, Gus Fetch liked to hang with his homeboys. Growing up in Compton he shared a bathroom with four sisters and a religious mother. He grew up yearning for his own place—and male companionship.

Today, his success as a private detective afforded him a house with four bathrooms and a den the size of a basketball court. *America is a great country,* Gus thought, surveying the fruits of his labor. Pinball machines and video games were available to his guests as were pool tables and a full bar. And Gus had plenty of guests. He saw himself as the black Hugh Hefner.

Gus knew that others saw him as an aggressive

bullying asshole who liked to throw his weight and money around to manipulate everyone around him. He had to admit they had a point. But Gus didn't care as long as he got what he wanted. Which was plenty.

*In Hollywood you need an entourage,* Gus reflected as he studied the reactions of his crew. They were slouched around his enormous TV drinking beer, eating chips and watching a tape of his greatest hits. Gus had edited some of his most bizarre footage into a fifty-minute video and it was getting good laughs all around. He ambled closer to the screen.

He heard distant bellows and screams from the TV and recognized the segment; Henry Nearhouse the Poultry Czar, with Lana Lamont. Gus had broken in through the kitchen and taped them smearing each other with whipped cream and chocolate syrup. *Freaky, funky and flat-out funny,* Gus thought proudly.

"Oh yo, baby, eat this," howled a lanky brother named Swami J. "Man, that's some crazy shit."

"Man, let's go back to the football game," someone whined.

"Kiss my ass!" Gus barked. The room fell silent.

"Its halftime, man," Swami J said. "This is good shit."

From the TV came the tinny sound of Gus's voice.

*I'm gonna nail your ass . . .*

"Hey Gussie," someone rumbled—a fat cat known as Heavy Bud. "Let's see that Rabinowitz tape again. It's mad hilarious."

"No—wait!" Gus said sharply. "This is the good part comin' up here."

He heard his private cell chiming and ignored it.

"Ya see there . . . she's lookin' for her panties, and *he's wearin' 'em!*"

The entire crew roared with laughter. Music to Gus's ears.

A female voice sliced through the testosterone. It was Leona, his personal assistant. "Gus! Miles Massey a' Massey, Myerson!"

"Ahh, get a number!" Gus yelled. He knew Massey was a heavy player but he was enjoying himself.

"It's about a job—tonight."

"Goddammit!" Gus said. But he knew he'd take the job. Somebody had to pay for the party. And his emergency fee was obscene. Anyway, when Miles Massey called, people listened.

*Shit rolls downhill,* Gus observed as he gathered up his battle gear. He wondered whose ass Miles

Massey wanted nailed, and why it was so damn important it be nailed tonight . . .

Miles had thought of everything.

He had the evening scheduled down to the final minute. Eight o'clock reservations at Flaubert's bistro and guest list at the Viper Room later, should it come to that.

Miles doubted it would come to anything. True, Rexroth's ex was beautiful, he told himself as he waited for her to arrive. But this was business. In fact it was beyond business. It was the greatest challenge of his legal career.

Miles picked up a spoon and smiled, checking his reflection. Still, Rexroth's ex was fantastic. He avoided using her name to maintain the proper emotional distance. A woman that lovely was dangerous.

A man in his position attracted an inordinate number of beautiful females—and Miles loved them all. But none lasted longer than a month or so. His profession had made him extremely cynical concerning relationships. However, as he edged closer to forty, Miles had become aware of an odd state of being.

For the first time in his life he had sporadic fantasies about settling down and perhaps raising a family. While he would never admit it—

especially to himself—deep down beneath the power and glory of his success, Miles was lonely.

*I'm going to keep it cordial—and on schedule,* Miles thought, checking his Rolex. She was late, all the better. More time for Gus Fetch to get in and get what he needed. Serenity, he reminded himself. Just chill and enjoy the evening.

And yet as the minutes passed, Miles found he was impatient to see her.

When Marilyn appeared the elegant room seemed to vibrate with her sensual energy. All heads turned to watch the exquisite female in scarlet and black glide past the tables.

Despite an effort to remain distant, Miles couldn't keep his eyes off her. He rose as she neared the table and took her hand. It was cool. Very cool.

"Ms. Rexroth, I'm delighted you decided to come." *In fact I was counting on it,* he thought, noting her stony expression.

Marilyn allowed the maitre d' to pull out her chair. "I must admit I was curious."

"Something to start?" the maitre d' inquired. "Some wine, perhaps?"

Miles looked at Marilyn. "Red?"

She shrugged. "French?"

Miles smiled suavely. "Bordeaux?"

Marilyn shrugged again. "Chateau Margaux?"

"Fifty-seven?"

Marilyn ignored the vintage. "Mr. Massey . . ." she began crisply.

Miles nodded at the maitre d', who bowed and withdrew. Then he turned to Marilyn and unleashed his supernova smile. "Your husband had told me you were the most beautiful woman he had ever seen, but I didn't expect you to be the most beautiful woman *I'd* ever seen."

"'Dismiss your vows, your feigned tears, your flattery, for where a heart is hard, they make no battery . . .'" she quoted, her voice low and playful.

Miles found it a charming combination. He propped his chin on one fist and studied her. "Simon and Garfunkel?"

A trace of a smile softened her ivory features. Before she could answer, the waiter arrived. Miles nodded when offered the cork and the waiter poured a taste of wine.

Miles took a long sip, his eyes on Marilyn. "'. . . whoever loved, who loved not at first sight?'" He nodded approval at the waiter, who poured two glasses.

"Now, now," Marilyn scolded, "you didn't ask me here to pick me up—you could be disbarred for that."

*I could be arrested for what I'm doing tonight,*

Miles mused. He gave Marilyn a boyish smile. "Maybe I'm reckless."

She drank her wine, eyes studying him over the rim of her glass. "What was your performance about this afternoon?"

He fielded the question smoothly. "Well . . ." he said, as if surprised by her assessment. "What did your lawyer say?"

Her eyes locked on his. "Freddy thinks you're a buffoon. He says you've been too successful. That you're bored, complacent and on your way down."

"But you don't think so," Miles said calmly.

Again, a smile flickered across her impervious expression. "How do you know?"

"Why would you be here?" As he drank his wine, Miles checked his watch. Gus Fetch should be in by now.

"Why did you ask me?"

"Can't I be curious?" Miles said.

She sat back and cocked her head. "About what?"

Miles found the pose quite fetching. He also realized she'd be hard to shake on the witness stand.

"Do you ever answer questions?" he asked lightly.

"Do you?"

The waiter appeared with the menus. Miles waved them away.

"I'll have the tournedos of beef," he said, still looking at Marilyn, "and the lady will have the same."

"I assume you're a carnivore," Miles said when the waiter left.

Her eyes had the cold glint of black diamonds. "Mr. Massey, you've no idea."

"Miles, please," he murmered. He reached out and took her hand. "Tell me about yourself."

Marilyn pulled her hand away. "All right, Miles, let me tell you everything you need to know. You may think you're tough, but I eat men like you for breakfast. I've invested five good years in my marriage to Rex. I've nailed his ass fair and square and now I'm going to have it stuffed and mounted and have my lady friends over to throw darts at it."

"Mmmn," Miles said knowingly. "Man hater, huh?"

For a second he thought she was going to throw her glass at him. But she sipped her wine and gave him a wicked smile. "People don't go on safaris because they hate animals."

*Tell that to the animals,* Miles thought. "So it was just a hunt—with a trophy at the end?"

Her expression didn't waver. "Nothing that

frivolous. This divorce means money. Money means independence. That's what I'm after. What are *you* after, Miles?"

"Oh, I'm a lot like you," he said truthfully. "Just looking for an ass to mount."

"Well, don't look at mine," she warned.

*Actually I am looking at it,* Miles reflected, sneaking a peek at his watch. He had to admit she was quite a remarkable woman. He almost felt guilty about duping her like this.

Almost, but not really. After all, he was the Terminator.

Gus Fetch regretted taking this gig.

First of all, there was no errant husband or wife to nail, which took all the fun out of it.

Instead there were those fucking dogs.

Wishing he had packed a gun, Gus crouched in the darkened hallway doing stretching exercises. *Got a cramp comin' on,* he thought bitterly. He tested his knee, the one he hurt playing linebacker at Grambling. It seemed all right. *You never know with this knee,* he brooded, stretching his legs from side to side. With his black leotards he might have been an Alvin Ailey dancer instead of a private eye facing felony burglary— and two vicious dogs.

Gus had gotten what he came for. Now he

needed to get back to his SUV with all his body parts. He had already hatched an escape plan. First he found some hamburger meat in the refrigerator. Then he opened the kitchen door, made some loud noises and flung a mass of ground meat into the darkness.

Gus could hear them snarling as he left the kitchen and headed for the front hall. After taking a few minutes to get loose, Gus inhaled deeply and opened the door.

He leaped past the fountain and hit the driveway at a dead sprint, chunky legs pumping under the weight of his backpack. But the dogs weren't fooled for long.

Halfway to the gate the rottweilers appeared, madly gleaming eyes and slavering fangs emerging from the shadows with only one purpose: to nail his breaking-and-entering ass.

Wheezing like a smoke alarm, Gus put on the afterburners. He managed a two-step surge but it was useless. He heard the snarling beasts gaining on him. There was only one chance.

With a gurgling cry, Gus leaped at the ten-foot iron fence surrounding the estate. By pure luck he managed to wrap both hands around one of the lower bars and pulled himself up—kicking and clawing until he managed to get one leg over the top of the gate.

Exhausted, he flopped weakly over the iron bar. Then he heard the growling. He opened his eyes and saw them circling below like four-legged sharks, fanged jaws snapping in gruesome anticipation.

Gus looked wistfully at the Mercedes SUV parked just outside the gate. So near, yet so fucking far. Maybe if he could shimmy along the fence and drop down on the roof. . . . Having no choice, Gus started inching his way across the bar. The dogs stayed right with him.

Gus made it about two feet when he felt the fence move. As he clung to the bar the gate slowly hinged open, leaving him suspended in space.

*I'm gonna die,* Gus ranted silently. *Chewed to death by vicious killer beasts. Won't be enough left to bury. Maybe my momma was right and they ain't dogs, but demons sent to punish me for being a world-class sinner.*

And for what? Nothing but some stupid, no-account address book.

Gus prepared himself, then reached into his pocket for the last of the hamburger. He waved it back and forth over the dog's snarling jaws, then threw it as far as he could. For an awful moment the dogs hesitated, then bounded off in search of their appetizer.

Awkwardly Gus half slid, half dropped to the ground. He started to run and thanked God as he neared the SUV. A moment later he heard the dogs snarling just behind him. He could hear their paws clawing frantically and thought he felt the heat of their muscular bodies. Desperately he lunged for the SUV door but it was too high. As he scrambled to climb inside he felt his knee pop.

At the same time one of the dogs clamped his jaw on Gus's good leg. Screaming, cursing and kicking wildly in pain and fear, Gus managed to slam the door. Without turning on his headlights he peeled out of there, denting his front fender in the process.

*Soon as I get my sorry ass home,* Gus swore grimly, *first damn thing I do—I'm gonna hit Miles Massey with the mother of all fees.*

Miles stood and began pacing back and forth. A faraway look came over his face—the look of a young Da Vinci envisioning human flight.

"So you propose that, despite demonstrable infidelity on your part, your unoffending wife should be tossed out on her ear?"

Something in the question gave Rex hope. "Well . . . is that possible?"

Miles stopped near a window overlooking the

hills. "It's . . ." He turned and beamed at Rex. ". . . it's a *challenge*."

Standing at the window awash in sunlight, Miles's smile flashed like white lightning. Suddenly the boredom, the angst evaporated. This case would be his greatest test.

Rex sat in silent awe sensing the transformation. For the first time since the black detective nailed him, he was able to think about playing night train again.

# CHAPTER
# EIGHT

The diner reeked of grease and cholesterol. The phony leather booths were tattered and the ketchup bottles had dirty red worms around the caps.

Wrigley suspiciously eyed the plate of greenish fries at the next table, then lifted his hand. A middle-aged waitress with hair like a brass helmet came over and brandished her check pad.

"Yeah?"

"I'll have a salad, please . . ." Wrigley scanned the menu and looked up. ". . . baby salad greens?"

The waitress stared at him. "What did you call me?"

"I . . ." Wrigley glanced at Miles, who looked elsewhere. ". . . I didn't call you anything."

"You wanna salad?"

"Oh yes, uh, do you have a green salad?"

She shook her head. "What the fuck color *would* it be?"

"Why are we eating here?" Wrigley hissed. "Why not Wolfgang's, or even Canter's?"

The waitress looked at Miles. "Whatsa matter with him?"

Miles flashed his salt-of-the-earth smile. "Heh-heh, just bring him some iceberg lettuce and a mealy tomato wedge smothered in French dressing."

"And for you?"

"Ham sandwich on stale rye. Lots of mayo, easy on the ham."

"Slaw cup?"

Miles tossed the menu aside. "What the hell."

As the waitress turned, a strange black man limped to the table and painfully sat down. Wrigley gaped in surprise but Miles seemed unperturbed.

"How are you, Gus?" the waitress said over her shoulder. "Usual?"

"Hello, Marge, make it the usual," Gus said. He looked at Miles and slid a roll of film across the table.

Grinning, Miles snatched it up and put it in his pocket.

Gus wasn't smiling as he leaned closer. "Okay, I Minoxed her address book but don't call me anymore for this penny-ante shit. I shoot *action!* Me and the Ikegami Jack!" He glared at Wrigley as if daring him to disagree.

"Thank you, Gus," Miles said politely.

But Gus wasn't through. "And those rottweilers were a menace, man."

"I told you she had dogs."

Gus slapped the table. "You didn't tell me they had a hard-on for Anus Africanus!"

"There'll be a bonus," Miles assured smoothly.

"Oh, I know that." Gus passed him an envelope. "My bill."

Miles looked at the figure and whistled softly. "Write him a check, Wrigley. Your name, not mine." He smiled at Gus. "Did you see any evidence, any telltale signs of . . . how shall I say, any indiscretions on the part of Mrs. Rexroth?"

Gus squinted at him like an indignant bulldog. "What the hell are you talkin' about, telltale signs? I see an ass, I nail it. I don't sneak around sniffin' the sheets. Goddammit, I'm Gus Fetch!"

"Uh, should I make this check out to you?" Wrigley inquired.

Later as he and Miles were walking to the car, Wrigley asked, "Just what did I pay for anyway?"

"You don't want to know."

"Actually, I do. What did he mean when he said he 'Minoxed her address book?'"

"A Minox is a tiny camera. Gus photographed Marilyn Rexroth's address book. She'll never know he was there."

Wrigley felt nauseous. The sour taste of French dressing burned his throat. "Couldn't you be disbarred for that?"

"Oh, I don't think so; maybe if I had ordered the patty melt."

"You had a guy break into her house and photograph her address book."

Miles paused. "Oh no, Wrigley. I happened to let a guy know that I was *interested* in her phone book. That's not criminal. I also let him know I was taking her out to dinner, but that's not a crime, either. No, I don't see myself as culpable in any sense."

He belched and handed Wrigley the film. "*You*, on the other hand, could be disbarred for developing and examining these pictures, but that really doesn't concern me." He turned and began walking.

Wrigley stayed with him. In the year he had been Miles's associate he had become inured to criminal behavior. He pulled out his Swiss Army phone. "Right. Who am I looking for?"

"Tenzing Norgay."

"Tenzing Norgay," he muttered, nodding. "Is that someone she slept with?"

"I doubt it," Miles said cheerfully. "Tenzing Norgay was the Sherpa who helped Edmund Hillary climb Mount Everest."

"And Marilyn knows him?"

Miles stopped. "No, you idiot—not *the* Tenzing Norgay. *Her* Tenzing Norgay."

Wrigley felt the nausea return. "I'm not sure I . . ."

Miles looked at him. His eyes had a messianic glaze as if he was delivering a message from above. "Few great accomplishments are achieved singlehandedly, Wrigley. Most have their Norgay. Marilyn Rexroth is even now climbing *her* Everest. I want to find her Tenzing Norgay."

Inadvertantly, Wrigley belched. The fetid odor of spoiled French dressing came up. Miles turned and marched to his Mercedes. Still confused by Miles's lofty concept, Wrigley ran after him.

As Miles got into his car Wrigley, held up the roll of film.

"But Miles—how do you determine which of the people in here . . . ?"

Miles shut the door and rolled down the window. "How do you spot a Norgay?"

"Yeah," Wrigley said, ready for the secret.

Miles motioned him closer. "Well, you start with the people with the funny names . . ."

He rolled down the window and pulled out of the lot, leaving Wrigley standing there. *Court date comes up in two days,* Wrigley thought, belching again. *I'd better get this developed.* He spotted Gus Fetch leaving the diner and scurried to the safety of his Saab.

"Oyez, oyez, family court for the fifth district of Los Angeles County is now in session . . ."

Miles always found the words an inspiration. He heard them as a clarion call to the battlefield of justice. Well, a battlefield anyway, he amended as they waited for the judge to enter.

Rex Rexroth sat between Miles and Wrigley. He was perspiring profusely in his unaccustomed suit and tie. In the weeks he'd been with Nina he had gotten used to his railroad overalls. Nina had also given him some pills to calm his nerves, but they seemed to be having the opposite effect. He tried not to look at Marilyn,

A large black woman in judicial robes entered from behind the Solomonic platform.

"The Honorable Marva Munson presiding," the clerk announced. "All rise."

Miles, Rex and Wrigley got to their feet and

respectfully faced forward. "Have you sat before her before?" Rex whispered.

"No, no, the judge sits first," Miles said out of the side of his mouth.

"Well, have you sat *after* her before?"

Wrigley leaned closer. "Sat after her before? You mean, have we argued before this judge?"

"So . . ." Rex persisted, "have you argued before her before?"

Wrigley and Miles glanced at each other. They had played this game with each other many times. It relieved the tedium of their long hours listening to irrelevant testimony. "Before *her* before?" Wrigley whispered. "Or before she *sat* before?"

Rex felt dizzy. "Before her before, I *said*, before her before."

"You said before she sat before."

"At first I did but then—" Rex looked to Miles for help.

Miles stared straight ahead. "Look, don't argue."

"I'm not," Rex whined, "I'm just . . ."

"You don't argue," Wrigley hissed. *"We* argue."

*"Counsel* argues," Miles said, smiling at the judge.

"You appear," Wrigley corrected.

Miles nodded. "The judge sits."

"Then you sit."

"That's right, or you'd stand in contempt."

Rex looked from Miles to Wrigley, sweat drenching his silk shirt.

"Then we argue," Wrigley said.

"*Counsel* argues," Miles reminded.

Rex blinked. "Which you've done before."

"Which we've done before," Miles assured, eyes on the judge.

"But not before her," Wrigley confided.

The gavel's *whack* ended all conversation. Everyone in the courtroom sat down except one person. Rex remained on his feet, staring straight ahead, as his numbed brain tried to digest what they told him.

Wrigley tugged his sleeve. "Rex! Sit!"

Rex slumped in his chair and loosened his tie a notch. *What difference did it make?* he thought grimly, resigned to his fate. Miles Massey might be the sharpest attorney in Hollywood, but the bottom line was Marilyn had the damned video. Once the jury saw that, he was roadkill.

And see it they did.

Rex took the opportunity to unbutton his shirt when the court darkened its lights. He watched the judge's face in the flickering light of the TV monitor and saw it grow stern. Faintly, leaking from the judge's earphones, came the tinny sound of those dread words.

Those words, that voice, drilled through his brain. Those words he'd heard over and over inside his head ever since that night. The night his life became a pile of dog shit, subjecting him to ruin and public ridicule.

*I'm gonna nail your ass!*

Rex heard a collective gasp and saw Marilyn, also wearing earphones, weeping delicately as she watched her monitor. Freddy Bender stood behind her, his consoling hand on her shoulder.

When the lights went on, the judge turned to glare at Rex. However, Miles seemed oblivious to the hostility generated by the video. Even when Freddy Bender put Marilyn, still sniffling, on the witness stand, then led her to the killing floor and put a knife in her hand— the better to skewer Rex—Miles offered no objection.

"Tell me, Ms. Rexroth, in your own words, how did this affect you?" Freddy said, sneering in Rex's direction.

Marilyn struggled for composure, her face the essence of wounded innocence. "Devastated," she said with a wrenching sob. "I was simply devastated."

"That will be all, Ms. Rexroth," Freddy said. He sighed sympathetically and nodded at the judge.

The sweat had soaked through Rex's socks by the time Bender was finished. Roadkill.

Judge Munson looked disapprovingly at Miles. "Mr. Massey, any questions?" Obviously she felt there was no need.

*Roadkill.*

Rex was glad Nina decided to stay home. Her home. He no longer had a home, or a bank account. His assets were frozen and his business tottered on the brink of annihilation.

Miles slowly got to his feet. "Yes, Your Honor, I do."

"Very well, you may proceed," Judge Munson said grudgingly. She checked her watch.

Marilyn buried her face in her handkerchief as Miles approached the witness stand. As if in deference to her suffering, he paced back and forth, brow furrowed in concern.

Finally, still pacing, Miles began to recite. " 'Dismiss your vows, your feigned tears, your flattery, for where a heart is hard, they make no battery.' "

Marilyn looked up in startled irritation. Miles stopped and turned to face her. "Do you know those lines, Ms. Rexroth?"

Her eyes narrowed as she studied him. Freddy saw something in her expression and sensed a threat. He leaped to his feet.

"Objection, Your Honor!"

The judge seemed mystified. "Grounds?"

Freddy blinked reflectively. "Uh . . . poetry recitation?"

"Let me rephrase," Miles said smoothly. "Ms. Rexroth, 'high is that wall around your heart'?"

"Objection," Freddy pleaded. "Your Honor, this is harassment! And it's still a little . . ." He fluttered his hand mockingly. ". . . artsy, fartsy."

Rex winced and gave Wrigley a doomed groan. To his surprise the modest, bespectacled associate returned a look of utter disdain. *Forgetaboutit*, the look said, *we've got it covered.*

Rex wondered if Massey, Myerson was a Mafia front, like in that Tom Cruise movie.

"Rephrase," Miles declared before the judge could sustain. "Ms. Rexroth, have you ever been in love?"

Marilyn glanced at Freddy, who lifted his brows as if to say *beats me*. "Of course, I've been in love with Rex."

Through his despair Rex felt a tingle. Maybe they could work it out, compromise, take train trips together.

However, Miles seemed skeptical. "And you've always loved him?"

A faint smile slipped across Marilyn's tear-streaked face. " 'Whoever loved, who loved not at first sight?' "

Miles returned a fleeting smile. "So your sworn testimony is, you loved Rex Rexroth since you first met?"

Marilyn eyed him suspiciously, then retreated behind her handkerchief and burst into sobs. She nodded her head emphatically, too helpless to speak.

"Thank you, Your Honor," Miles said softly. "No further questions."

*That's it?* Rex thought. *At the rate I'm paying, that's a hundred grand a question!* His doubts returned in the form of a violent itching on his ankles and scalp.

As a bailiff assisted Marilyn—still weeping—from the stand, the judge turned to Freddy. "Who's next, Mr. Bender?"

Freddy spread his arms in a Christ-like pose. "We rest, Your Honor."

"Mr. Massey?"

Miles smiled regretfully. He shifted his shoulders like a man weighed down by a moral burden. "Your Honor, I call Heinz, the Baron Krauss von Espy."

"Heinz, the Baron Krauss von Espy," the bailiff called out.

A bailiff at the far door repeated the call. "Heinz, the Baron Krauss von Espy," he shouted into the hallway.

Wrigley smirked knowingly and leaned closer to Rex. "Tenzing Norgay," he whispered. Rex gaped at him.

Marilyn stopped in midsob and stared at the door apprehensively. Freddy Bender noticed her reaction. "Problem?"

"Puffy," she said absently.

"Did you sleep with him?" Freddy asked.

"Don't be a fool!" she hissed.

Her intensity worried Freddy. A sense of impending disaster swept over him. He'd had the same feeling during the Guttman case. He tried to calm down.

*It's a ploy,* Freddy told himself. *What could happen? We have the video. His ass is officially nailed.* He felt better when he saw the witness Miles had called walk into the courtroom.

Rex, on the other hand, felt worse. Nina's pills had really taken effect. His brain was whirring like a helicopter inside his skull while his heartbeat skipped from rapid-fire bursts to sporadic pops. *I know that man from somewhere.*

The man Miles had called as his witness had

slicked-back hair and the suave good looks of a gigolo. He was dressed in a black jacket, blue shirt and pink ascot and carried a small Pomeranian dog. The dog yapped as the man strolled to the witness stand.

When he was settled the bailiff held out the Bible. "Uh, Mr. . . . Krauss, do you—"

"Krauss von Espy," the man corrected. The dog yapped.

"Mr. Krauss von Espy, do you—"

"*Baron* Krauss von Espy," the man said modestly. The dog yapped.

The bailiff didn't miss a beat. "Do you solemnly swear that the testimony you are about to give shall be the truth, so help you God?"

"*Mais bien sûr.*"

Judge Munson shook her head. "No maybes."

"*Mais bien sûr*—but of course," he explained with a wounded smile. "The Baron does not lie."

The dog yapped. "Shhh, Elisbieta . . ." Krauss cooed, "shushy, shush, shush. We are in court now. See the nice judge . . ."

"Can't we object? The dog . . . ?" Marilyn whispered.

"Won't happen," Freddy said mournfully. Lot of pets passed through family court in Hollywood. Dogs, cats, birds, tigers; one client had even insisted on bringing her pet python to the proceedings. Unfortunately the snake got loose and swallowed the judge's Chihuahua. Fortunately for Freddy, it wasn't his client. He won a huge settlement. *Maybe the dog is a sign,* Freddy thought.

"Now Baron von Espy," Miles said briskly, "what is your profession?"

Krauss laughed airily and waved his free hand. "Silly man, I am a baron."

Miles nodded. "But uh, Baron, do you not also hold a day job?"

Krauss seemed confused.

"Uh . . . a paying job, a square job?" Miles clarified.

Krauss looked at the judge. "Well, one has to live. I am the concierge of Les Pantalons Rouges at Bad Godesberg in the Canton of Uri." The dog yapped.

"Baron, tell me." Miles smiled, as if they were sharing a carafe of wine in some bistro. "What does your job entail?"

"I satisfy such requests as the clientele may present," Krauss said loftily.

"Towels, ice, et cetera?"

"We have bellmen for that." Krauss sniffed indignantly. "No, no, such requests that, were you at home, you would address not to your valet—but your majordomo." He smiled at the judge. The dog yapped.

"Shush, poochy—chow."

"I see . . . Baron, do you recognize that woman?" Miles pointed at Freddy Bender's table.

Krauss produced a monocle, screwed it in his eye and peered across the room. "Cher Marilyn—but of course."

Freddy peeked at his client. Marilyn Rexroth dabbed at her tear-stained face but her handkerchief concealed an expression of cold fury.

"She was a guest at the uh, Red, uh, Trousers Chalet?"

"Oh, many times," Krauss assured. "For relaxing and making Alpine recreation."

"I am curious about your visit of five years ago—January of 1998," Miles went on easily,

Freddy saw Marilyn stiffen and press the handkerchief against her mouth. A trickle of sweat began snaking down the back of his neck.

"Do you happen to remember any specific requests?" Miles continued. "Requests she might have made on that visit?"

"Yes, I do."

Through his medicated haze Rex finally remembered Kraussy from that damned Kraut ski resort. Kraussy, who told everyone at the hotel Rex was a "choo-choo-cuckoo." Now he was about to do it again—on the record. He had to warn Miles somehow. He tapped Wrigley's sleeve but the associate shook him off.

"Not now," Wrigley hissed vehemently.

"And what did she, at that time, tell you she required?" Miles continued.

Krauss nuzzled his dog. "She said that she required—" he paused and looked at Marilyn—"a husband."

The courtroom began to buzz and the dog yapped fiercely.

"Oh, do you want some Bonz?" Krauss asked the dog, "Does Elisbieta want some Bonz?" He glanced around. "Has anyone any Bonz?"

The dog kept yapping. Amid the confusion, Freddy felt his stomach churn.

Miles turned to the gallery, ever the smiling champion of animal rights. "Does anyone have any Bonz?" he asked, unable to mask his irritation. "Uh, dog candies?"

"They are not candies!" Krauss objected. "Milk Bonz! Hard, crunchy bone things—for the teeth!"

"I—we don't seem to have any," Miles said soothingly. "We will attend to the dog later. Now . . ." He tried to retrace his train of thought but it had disappeared.

Miles turned to the court reporter. "I'm sorry—where were we?"

The reporter spooled up her tape and began reading. " 'She said that she required—a husband. Oh, do you want some Bonz? Does Elisbieta want some Bonz?' "

"Yes, thank you," Miles said, back on track. "Now a husband—this is an unusual request. Did she specify what kind of husband she was looking for?"

Marilyn tensely jabbed her attorney's arm. "Freddy—stop him!"

Freddy jumped to his feet. "Objection!"

"Grounds?" the judge inquired.

"Uh . . . hearsay."

Miles approached the bench. "Not second-hand, Your Honor. This is direct testimony about the baron's own conversation."

Judge Munson nodded. "I'm going to allow it."

Hand still raised and hopes sinking, Freddy sat down. Marilyn glared at him from behind her handkerchief as Krauss went on.

"She said she wanted a very rich husband. She wanted to know the businesses and the wealths—the wealths?" He looked at Miles. "Can I say this, wealths . . . ?" The dog yapped. "Of our various eligible guests."

Miles seemed both surprised and fascinated. "Did she have any other qualifications?"

*Oh no,* Freddy thought, *there's more?* He lunged out of his chair. "Objection, Your Honor!" he called out desperately. "Inflammatory!"

"What's good for the gander, Your Honor," Miles declared.

Trembling, Rex stared balefully at the effete fop on the witness stand.

"Is this a legal argument," Freddy demanded, " 'what's good for the gander'?"

Miles was the picture of fairness. "Freddy," he reminded calmly, "you got to show your tape."

"Mr. Massey has a point there," Judge Muson conceded. "I'm going to allow it."

Wrigley turned to wink but Rex's attention was fixed on the witness. Rex knew what Kraussy was up to. Kraussy was going to humiliate him in public.

"What, then, were her other specifications?" Miles asked.

"She specificated a *silly* man."

"Your Honor!" Freddy pleaded. "Objection!"

Blithely, the witness went on. "She specificated a man who, though clever at making money, would be easily duped and controlled."

"Objection, Your Honor," Freddy yelled, his voice drenched with outrage.

Miles turned. "Oh, shut up, Freddy, she's allowing it!"

"She specificated a man with a wandering peepee," Krauss confided. "How you say, a philanderer—whose affairs would be transparent to the world!"

"Objection, Your Honor," Freddy said weakly. He felt his own world crumbling, destroyed by Miles Massey.

But Krauss wasn't finished. "And finally, a man whom she could herself brazenly . . ."

He lifted his index finger to the side of his head to make the classic sign of the horns. ". . . cuckold! Until such time as she might choose to—oh, we say *fair un coup de matteau sur des fesses*—you would say, make hammer on his fanny."

Above the buzzing voices the dog began yapping louder. It hopped frantically in the baron's lap, nipping at his face.

A raging curtain dropped over Rex's numbed brain. The bastard was doing it again.

"Objection!" Freddy repeated lamely. "Irrelevant!"

"I'm going to allow it," the judge droned.

Miles raised his voice a notch, going in for the kill. "Tell us, Baron! Did you introduce her to such a man?"

"Sir!" Krauss drew himself up proudly. "I was—the concierge."

Miles's voice boomed. "And to whom did you introduce that calculating woman?"

"I introduced her to . . . *that* silly man!" Krauss pointed at Rex as the courtroom erupted. The dog yapped louder.

Freddy lurched to his feet. "Objection!"

"Let the record show that the baron has identified Rex Rexroth as the silly man!" Miles declared.

The statement was the last straw. Rex slowly got to his feet, yanking at his tie. Swaying in front of his chair, he glared at Krauss through glazed, red-rimmed eyes.

The courtroom was buzzing loudly. Many of the spectators were muttering into cell phones. As the dog yelped furiously, Krauss half rose from his chair, swept up by the crescendo of noise and excitement he had created.

"I introduced her to that silly man!" he shouted, his voice laced with hysteria.

Rex could stand it no longer. "You son of a bitch!" he cried, charging at the witness stand. "They call *me* sick? I didn't use anyone, did I?" he screamed, wrapping his hands around the baron's throat. "I just like *trains!*"

The baron started to gurgle through his constricted throat. "If you please, sir . . . not the larynx!"

"Objection, Your Honor," Freddy shouted. "Strangling the witness!"

The judge tossed her gavel aside.

"I'm going to allow it."

# CHAPTER
# NINE

A week after the trial Rex moved back into his house.

He had settled out of court with the baron, sending him back to Europe with a tidy tithe. But it was all worth it; Massey's enormous fee, the public disclosures, the grief.

Miles had struck a blow for all men, Rex gloated, checking to make sure the dogs were gone. As if a curse had been lifted, his real estate deal had begun to jell. But even better than the money was the vindication of his sexuality—and the sweet revenge.

Instead of being labeled a perverted, pampered playboy, his beautiful and intelligent ex-wife had been exposed as a scheming bitch bent on stealing his fortune. *History is written by the winners,* Rex observed.

The first thing he planned to do was redecorate the place. Nina wanted him to wait until she moved in, of course, but there were a couple of items he needed to handle personally.

Rex found a hammer and nails and went to the foyer. A large, framed piece was leaning against the wall, next to the fountain. He fitted the piece, banged in a nail and hung it up.

It was perfect. There in the entrance, for all to see, was a life-size photographic portrait of his hero—Miles Massey—the man who saved his ass.

His other project was a bit more ambitious.

Rex made himself a drink and gazed fondly at the rolling lawns outside his window.

When the money from this deal came in, he intended to build a miniature railroad that would start at the entrance gate, and curve around the entire estate, from the pool to the tennis court. It would transform his world into an erotic terminal, with Nina as his dispatcher.

As he stood admiring the sunset, Rex shivered at the sheer magnitude of his fantasy.

His own railroad—just like Michael Jackson.

Marilyn liked to think of herself as a realist.

She had worked her way through high school

and managed to get a scholarship to Sarah Lawrence. After that her natural beauty acquired her a succession of college beaus, each richer and more accomplished than the last. Through them she learned how to ride horses, drive sports cars, drink fine wine, and distinguish herself in sophisticated circles.

However, for lessons in love she preferred older, more experienced men. Perhaps because she never really knew her father. It didn't matter. Marilyn didn't waste time thinking about why she did things, she just did them. And when it came to men, she did plenty.

Marilyn had a healthy appetite for life but upon graduation, she found it wasn't a level playing field. It was clear that to achieve the life she dreamed of, she needed to work out an alternative plan.

It soon became clear that marriage was the answer. Marilyn liked men. She just didn't like the men she married. A trait that made it easier to execute her divorce settlements.

Her first two husbands had been mere stepping stones to Rex Rexroth, she reflected with a trace of bitterness. Rex was the big score, the one that would give her the independence to find her place in the world, and maybe even find a real relationship.

But Miles Massey had taken care of all that.

*How in hell did he dig up Puffy?* Marilyn wondered as she pulled her suitcases from the trunk and followed Sarah to the pool house.

"It's perfect for you," Sarah was saying. "Your own little cottage, come and go as you please. Ta-daa . . ." She opened the door and stepped aside to let Marilyn enter. ". . . just like O.J."

Marilyn shrugged and went over to one of the beds. She dropped her bags and looked around.

Sarah shook her head sympathetically. "I think it stinks. They left you with absolutely nothing! It makes you wonder about the entire legal system . . ."

"They bought Massey's argument," Marilyn sighed. "If I lied and cheated and was only in it for Rex's money, he shouldn't have to give it to me."

"That makes no sense. Why else would you put in all those years?" Sarah checked her reflection in the mirror. "Anyway—*aghhhhh* . . ."

Grimacing, she doubled over and sat heavily on the bed, clutching at her side.

"Sarah? Are you all right?" Marilyn said, alarmed by her friend's obvious pain.

She nodded, trying to catch her breath. "I—yes—I . . ."

Marilyn bent closer. "What is it? Can I get you anything?"

"Peptic ulcer." Sarah took a deep breath. "I have medication but sometimes it doesn't . . ."

Marilyn hugged her gently. "You shouldn't be living alone, Sarah."

"My goddamn husbands *gave* me this ulcer."

"But a bottle of Bromo can't love you back."

Love. Both women reacted to it, Sarah with a sneer of hatred and Marilyn with fear. *When did love become such a scary word?* Marilyn thought, her concern for Sarah deepened by sadness.

"Yeah it's a catch-twenty-two," Sarah groaned. "I have to admit I don't like living alone. Do I really need forty-six rooms?"

"Well, you can see people; you don't have to live like a monk."

"Ahh, it's risky. Palimony, the sonuvabitch Marvin Mitchelson." She lowered her voice and leaned closer. "I'm telling you, honey, getting laid is financial Russian roulette."

Sarah massaged her stomach. "Maybe I'll just tear it all down, put up a cottage, twenty rooms. With my money I can't risk fooling around with the creeps in this town." She beamed at Marilyn. "And I've got you. It'll be fun, just the girls."

Marilyn managed a weak smile. "Thanks, but I can't sleep on your couch forever."

She gazed out the open door to the pool beyond as if looking into a crystal ball. "I'm going to marry again, and nail the guy's ass good," she said, almost to herself.

Marilyn had been working on this little project since the trial.

While at Sarah Lawrence, Marilyn had spent her junior year in Paris, where she had an affair with Alain, a handsome French rogue who happened to be a master jewel thief.

Alain was also a brilliant strategist and con man. He conceived blueprints for perfect crimes, each more ingenious than the last. Of all her lovers, Alain had been her most inspiring mentor.

And Marilyn had put everything she had ever learned—from Alain and from life—into devising a plan to snatch Miles Massey's family jewels.

Her face became a grim mask of determination. "And this time there won't be any Puffy von Espy."

The very next day Marilyn put on a Jil Sanders suit and drove to downtown Los Angeles. She parked her BMW and strolled a few blocks, checking the street signs against the one listed on her Palm Pilot. Finally she found it—Paradise.

Although officially billed as a street, Paradise was a garbage-strewn alley behind a Mexican restaurant.

As Marilyn entered she was aware of a strange stench, unlike any she had encountered. *Might be a corpse,* she speculated. *Or just some bad burritos.*

Moving deeper into the alley, she came to the conclusion that it was deserted. She would have to return at another time, perhaps at night. She had been informed noon and midnight were the best hours.

She turned to leave and noticed a pile of garbage against the wall. Two legs protruded from the pile. *The corpse, no doubt,* she speculated darkly. *Certainly has the right cologne,* she noted, moving closer. The corpse was wearing a Bruno Magli on one foot and a Gucci on the other. Then she saw something else.

Sticking up from the top of the pile was something that resembled a TV aerial. Gingerly, Marilyn leaned forward and peeled away the layers of newspaper. The first thing she saw was that the TV aerial was actually the tip of a gold sword on some sort of trophy. Marilyn read the inscription: DAYTIME TELEVISION LIFETIME ACHIEVEMENT AWARD.

The next thing she saw was Donovan Donnelly.

The ruddy, confident face she had seen in last year's *People* magazine was now prematurely liver-spotted and grizzled by a dirty, ragged beard.

Deeply asleep, he clutched his award like a teddy bear.

"Excuse me, uh . . . excuse me, Mr. Donnelly?"

No answer; he didn't even seem to be breathing.

Marilyn nudged him hard with the toe of her Manolo Blahnik and he snuffled. She nudged him harder.

"Excuse me, Mr. Donnelly?" she said, prodding him into reluctant wakefulness.

"In a meeting," he croaked, eyes closed.

"Mr. Donnelly, my name is Marilyn Rexroth."

"Tied up," he rasped. "Have to return. Sorry."

"I need to speak with you now," Marilyn said firmly.

He didn't stir. "Have you an appointment?"

"Ah—yes, I have an appointment." She nudged him again.

"I'll be there shortly."

With great effort the frayed, shambling figure pulled himself up against the wall, hawked up a wad of black phlegm and opened his eyes, squinting painfully in the daylight. He turned and looked at her through narrow slits.

"So you are . . . ?" He looked at his wrist, elaborately focusing. "My eleven-thirty?"

She noticed he didn't have a watch. "Yes, my name is Marilyn Rexroth."

"Referred by?"

"Bunny Bartigan told me where to find you."

Donovan looked around bleakly. "And where is that?"

"I need . . ."

"Did Bunny also tell you, madam, that I was not always . . . as you see me now?" Donovan caressed his trophy.

"Yes—up until your divorce. That's why I'm here, I—"

Donovan fixed her with a sly, bleary stare. "In that case, may I trouble you for the price of a bottle of Chateau Grand Lafitte '87, north vineyard?"

"No, I—"

"South vineyard?"

"I'm sorry, I'd—"

"Eighty-eight?"

"No, you see I need—"

"Good God, madam," Donovan said, addressing the figure on his trophy. "What would you have me drink?"

"Mr. Donnelly, you used to know a lot of people. I'll be happy to help you, but first—I need a name."

Donovan looked puzzled. "You led me to believe you had one."

"No, you see, I need your help to take revenge on someone. Someone who deserves it."

"And who might that be?"

"Miles Massey."

The transformation was miraculous. At the mention of the divorce attorney's name, Donovan Donnelly sat up and opened his eyes. Their rheumy glaze was displaced by a fiery glint and his features hardened.

"Madam, you have my undivided attention. Hold all my calls."

# CHAPTER
# TEN

Miles had redecorated his office.

Everything was now transparent. The desk, the bar, the tables, the TV and stereo; even the files were encased in glass or Lucite. It had been featured in last month's issue of *World of Interiors* as a "bold American statement."

Miles stood at the window, gazing out at the Hollywood Hills as he spoke rapidly into a microcassette recorder.

"And of course, we will have to litigate. Sentence. Paragraph."

He paused for a long moment, then went on. "Naturally the first concern for both parties is the welfare of little Wendell Junior." *The brat is slightly to the right of the Menendez brothers,* Miles observed silently.

"Nevertheless we question whether the continuing expenses for his special ed classes are truly justified given the great strides—"

The intercom buzzed. "Mr. Massey," a voice said, "Mr. Myerson wonders if you have a moment."

Miles was flabbergasted. "Herb wants to see me?"

"If you have a moment."

A moment? Miles had seen the founder of Massey, Myerson exactly two times. The first when he joined the firm, the second when he was made a partner and the third when he visited Herb in the hospital.

Herb Myerson was a fabulous legal figure whose victories had set historic precedents. Herb Myerson had rewritten California divorce law. Herb Myerson owned two hotels in Las Vegas.

He was also a legendary recluse in the tradition of Howard Hughes, Miles reflected, strolling down the long hall. It was whispered that Herb had the president's cell number. But Herb's number was private.

Miles wondered why Herb had called him. He mentally shuffled possibilities. Nothing paired up. He girded himself and opened the oak door to Herb Myerson's sanctum.

Inside it was dark. The curtains were drawn

and the lights dim, Miles entered the enormous room and peered through the gloom. He made out the figure of an ancient man—small and hunched—seated behind a huge desk.

Coming closer, Miles could see an odd gallows shape beside the seated figure. It was tall, thin and had something hanging from it. He realized it was an IV unit. A plastic tube snaked down into the old man's suit sleeve.

A voice began to speak—fragile, dry, lightly accented of a long-gone Brooklyn boyhood. The voice seemed disembodied and sourceless, as if it was the voice of the gloom itself.

". . . Twelve cawt days on the Rexrawt case alone," the voice wheezed. "Tree hunnut 'n twenty billable hours paralegal services; faw hunnut 'n two billable associate counsel and consultative; six hunnut 'n eighty billable at full attorney rate 'n eighty-five lunches charged."

A parched, withered hand, roped with veins, emerged from the gloom. It dangled like a dry leaf about to fall.

Miles took the offered hand. It was cold.

"Counseluh, you are the engine that drives this foim." The wheezing figure sat back, tongue flicking over his crusted lips.

For a few long seconds, Miles couldn't answer.

"Thank you, Herb," he said finally.

*The engine that drives this firm.* As Miles walked back to his office he didn't know if it was a compliment—or a curse.

For the rest of the afternoon Miles remained at his desk, fingers steepled, staring into space. He had just had a grotesque glimpse of his own bleak life, and his empty future.

Ironically, Miles had wanted this since high school. He had worked his way through college, earned a scholarship to Columbia Law School and set out to become the best attorney in the country. But not as a civil rights attorney defending the oppressed, Miles brooded. Not as a criminal attorney defending the innocent. No, he had turned out to be the most vicious fish in the pond. A divorce attorney, preying on the distressed emotions of the rich, the pampered and the pompous.

*I may as well be a damn Pekingese dog,* Miles sighed mournfully.

And even worse, he had nothing outside his work. The reason he stood on top of the Hollywood trash heap was because he had sacrificed his life, his time, his relationships, his happiness—whatever it took.

He had lied, cheated, cut corners, broken the law, all in the name of winning. *And what did I win?*

he asked himself. The chance to end up like Herb Myerson, a living mummy kept alive by an IV and pure greed: alone, unloved and unloving.

*You are the engine that drives this firm* was the closest thing to a human emotion Herb had ever expressed.

Miles could see his future stretched out before him like the Mars desert, barren and surreal.

His brooding was interrupted by the intercom. "Mr. Massey?"

"Please. No calls," he groaned. "I'm feeling very fragile." *Very lost is more like it,* he thought.

"I'm sorry, Mr. Massey, but I feel certain you'd want to know: Marilyn Rexroth wants to see you."

The effect was electric. Miles felt a mild shock run from belly to brain, deleting all rational thought. "Mnn . . . Marilyn Rexroth? When does she want to speak to—"

"She's here now."

The three simple words fell on him like a crumbling glacier.

He felt cold and hot at the same time. The combination induced a steamy sweat which dampened his shirt. Miles looked around, disoriented and vaguely panicked. "Is she armed?" he asked lightly. "Hah, hah, hah . . ." It sounded like he was coughing.

"Uh, give me a minute," he said finally. He hurried into his private bathroom. He considered taking a quick shower, then realized he was overdoing it. Miles settled for running a bit of gel through his hair and rinsing his face with cold water. Refreshed but far from serene, he stood in front of the mirror practicing.

"Marilyn, how nice to . . ." He shook his head and began again, pitching his voice lower. "Marilyn how lovely to, uh . . ."

He paused to run a finger across his teeth, which squeaked. Then he put on a suave smile. "Marilyn! What a pleasant . . ."

He left the bathroom, went to his desk and jabbed the intercom. "Janice, please send Ms. Rexroth in. And, uh, hold my calls."

Smiling suavely, Miles opened the door. "Marilyn! What a pleas—who the fuck are *you?*"

Standing in the doorways was a rugged, middle-aged man wearing a blue business suit and a large, gray cowboy hat. He gave Miles a toothy grin. Marilyn Rexroth was just behind him. She looked stunning.

"Miles, how nice of you to see us," she said smoothly. "May I introduce Howard D. Doyle of Doyle Oil?"

Before he could answer, Doyle grabbed his hand and pumped it enthusiastically, causing

Miles's body to waggle. *Does this bumpkin think I'm an oil well?* Miles thought.

"Goddamn glad to meet you," Doyle boomed. "Marilyn says you're the best. Just aces."

He jerked his hand back, teeth fixed in a fierce smile. "Er, yes, well, thank you, Mr., uh— are you by any chance related to John D. Doyle of Doyle Oil?"

"Yeah," Doyle said modestly. "Grampa John, I guess you mean. My pop was John D. Two— the Deuce, we called him, he was kinda the rebel a' the family." He beamed at Marilyn. "Knocked off the whole John D. routine when he christened little ol' yours truly Howard D. and Grampa nearly had a stroke. Well, a course he *did* have a stroke, but that was later, during the labor activity in '52 when the government stepped in—they called it 'mediation'; incipient communism, Grampa John called it, and that's when he had his—"

"Well, this is fascinating, Mr., uh, Doyle," Miles said briskly, trying to regain control. "But, uh, won't you have a seat?"

Doyle seemed mildly confused. "Seat? Oh, thanky, don't mind if I do." He looked around and settled on an inflated plastic sofa, sinking in so that his knees were at the level of his chin. He took a deep breath of relief.

"Marilyn had me runnin' up and down Rodeo Drive all day—kinda hit and run shoppin'; take no prisoners, forced march kinda thing and brother, are my dogs barkin'," Doyle confided genially. "We started at the damndest place down there near Wilshire . . ."

Marilyn sat in an Italian Lucite chair and looked at Miles. "Yes. It's been quite a day. Miles, I know you're busy—and charge by the hour—so I'll come to the point. Howard D. and I are planning to marry."

It was all Miles could do to keep his mouth from dropping open. He remained visibly composed, but his chest was cold and his neck was hot. He felt a trickle of sweat run down his rib cage. Finally he smiled.

"Well, well, uh . . . I suppose congratulations are in order."

"Well, thanky, Miles," Doyle said with a dreamy grin. "Yeah, the urge to wedlock, to form a monogamous bond sanctified by ritual seems to be pure nigh universal. Fact, it might innarest you to know, bein' in a related business, that even the Native Americans, matter of fact I believe it was the Cree—"

Marilyn sweetly interrupted. "The reason Howard and I are here, Miles, is because I have learned through bitter experience that when it

comes to matrimonial law, you are the very best."
She flashed an admiring smile.

Miles acknowledged the compliment with a
curt nod, but inwardly he was a writhing bundle
of conflicting emotions. *Did I drive her to this?* he
speculated wildly.

"As you are well aware," Marilyn continued
calmly, "my previous marriage ended with an
unjustified stain on my reputation. My motives
were impugned. I was slandered in court. I was
painted a harlot," she added, glancing at the
couch.

Doyle scowled and shook his head, as if unable
to believe man's inhumanity to woman. "Aw,
honey, I—"

"So I wish to execute a prenuptial agreement," Marilyn said flatly.

"I'm against it!" Doyle called out. "I'm four-
square, dead-set anti on this particular—"

"Howard's lawyers prefer it, and I *insist* on it,"
Marilyn declared.

"Aww, lawyers." Doyle made a dismissive gesture. "No offense."

Marilyn kept her eyes on Miles. "Now, it is my
understanding that the Massey prenup has
never been penetrated?"

"That is correct," Miles said, trying to appear
modest despite the fact that it remained his

greatest achievement. "Not to blow my own horn, but they devote an entire semester to it at Harvard Law."

"Do they now?" Doyle sounded impressed. " 'Course they got a helluva school up there—we gave 'em the Doyle Building a few years back—but I myself went to Texas A and M—that's right, I'm an Aggie."

Miles half expected him to wave a pennant and sing the school fight song. "Business?" he inquired politely.

Doyle winked. "No, tight end. I had a fair amount of success against the split-T defense 'cause when they line up all symmetrical like that—"

*She wants to marry this oaf?* Miles ranted inwardly. "If I may cut in," he said aloud, looking at Marilyn.

"Oh, I don't stand on ceremony," Doyle said cheerfully.

Miles kept looking at Marilyn. "I just want to make sure that you both understand what you're asking for here."

After a significant pause, he went on. "The Massey prenup provides that in the event of a dissolution of the marriage *for any reason,*" Miles paused again, eyeing her, "both parties shall leave it with whatever they brought in, and earned during. No one can profit from the marriage. The prenup protects the wealthier party"—he smiled at Doyle—"without it, that party is exposed, a sitting duck."

Doyle sat up. "Hell, there ain't a lot of romance in that!"

"No sir, there is not," Miles said, his belly churning. "No romance, and more to the point—no wriggle room. So . . ."

Miles paused once again, his eyes on Marilyn. "Are we both sure that's what we want?"

Marilyn looked from Doyle to Miles, her face glowing.

"Absolutely. It's my gift to Howard for my peace of mind—whether or not it worries him at the moment." She looked back at Doyle adoringly.

"Haw, haw, haw," Doyle brayed, winking at Miles. "Do I look worried?"

Miles felt like he was about to throw up. The single question—*How could she love this underbred lout?*—kept looping around his brain as he ushered them out to the elevator.

He pressed the button for them, then snapped his fingers. "Gosh, Ms. Rexroth, I almost forgot." He smiled at Doyle. "Excuse me, Mr. Doyle, if I could just borrow your charming fiancée for a moment?"

"Hell, okay, if you're gonna leave a deposit! Haw, haw!"

Miles took Marilyn's elbow and firmly steered her toward a spare office nearby. Behind them he could hear Doyle whistling "Turkey in the Straw."

"What are you up to?" he hissed as he half dragged her inside and closed the door.

"Something you wouldn't understand," Marilyn said huskily. She slowly backed up as he moved closer. "Howard D. and I are very much in love."

Miles found it impossible to believe. "I don't know what you're thinking, but I warn you, the Massey prenup has never been penetrated."

She accepted the news with a bored smile. "Thank you for your professional help." She started to leave, but Miles cut her off. "Marilyn, think of me for a moment not as an attorney, but as a friend."

"Does that mean you won't be billing us for this hour?" she murmered with a playful smile. There was an unspoken challenge in her upturned chin, her long-legged stance like a gunfighter's. Miles was aware of a current between them, and he was certain she felt it as well.

"Dump him! You can't nail his ass," he blurted, moving closer.

Her smile held a trace of disappointment. "Is that all?" she said coolly.

Miles had backed her up to the wall. He could feel the heat generated by their bodies flaring up. "No," he said hoarsely, "that's not all . . ."

Miles leaned closer and kissed her. As their lips met, he felt a small shock of recognition that grew in intensity. Her lips were moist and her breath steamy. Miles felt slightly dizzy.

As they slowly separated, Marilyn looked at him with an amused but detached expression. "I could have you disbarred for that."

"It was worth it."

The detached expression softened a notch. Her fingertips gently brushed his cheek. "A romantic divorce attorney," she whispered.

Smiling, she slid past him and walked away. When their bodies touched, Miles felt more than a small shock. It was like bumping a power line, sending a jolt of sensual energy straight up his spine.

"You fascinate me," Miles murmured as she opened the door.

Her tinkling laughter drifted back to him like smoke. It lingered long after she was gone.

# CHAPTER
## ELEVEN

Miles was spending a rare day at his mansion, enjoying the tennis court. However, even while jogging across the court—returning the balls hit by Niki, his nubile tennis pro—Miles had a cell phone glued to his ear.

He had stepped up the pace during the last few weeks, trying to keep Marilyn off his mind. But it was impossible. She was the first thing he thought of in the morning, the last thing at night. Miles couldn't stand it.

*How could she love a dope like Doyle?* kept revolving around his brain like a blimp at a football game.

Niki smacked a sharp backhand but Miles ran it down, the phone pressed against his ear. He ignored Niki's nasty glare as he hit the ball back to the corner.

Stubbornly, Niki chased the ball and somehow managed to lob it high, giving her time to get set. It infuriated her that Miles was able to sustain a volley while maintaining a phone conversation. It also annoyed her that Miles was oblivious to her very short shorts.

"Yes, all right," Miles said, swatting the ball into Niki's court. "I suppose so." He scurried forward and dropped Niki's return over the net. "Yes, I'll whip something up."

With one hand he flipped the phone shut and tossed it to Wrigley, who was lounging on the linesman's chair. With the other he blocked Niki's desperate lunging shot.

Wrigley watched in total awe of his boss's ability to multitask. He had dressed for the occasion in white boating pants, white commodore's cap and a white T-shirt with OBJECTION! blazoned across the front in slashing red letters.

"How's Lionel?" Wrigley asked, putting the phone in his pocket.

"Oh, fine." Miles sliced a low, curving ball at Niki's feet. "He just asked me to deliver the keynote address at this year's convention in Vegas."

Niki hopped to one side and scooped the ball over his head.

Wrigley doffed his cap. "That's quite an honor."

Miles hit the ball with his back to the net. It barely cleared. "Mnn, I suppose," he said without enthusiasm. *How could she love a dope like Doyle?*

"On top of a great victory," Wrigley prompted.

Niki got to the return and flipped it into midcourt.

"Oh? What was that?" Miles smoothly hit a forehand into the far corner, but Niki was already there, pro that she was. Miles had managed to ignite her competitive rage.

"What was that?" Wrigley rolled his eyes skyward. "Rex Rexroth! He kept everything! You won—no compromise. Isn't that what you wanted?"

Niki smacked a low, skipping shot that cut away, but Miles flicked a backhand. "Mnn, I suppose so."

"Good God, Miles—what are you looking for?"

It was a fine question—the one he'd been asking himself for months. "I don't know," Miles grunted. He swiped Niki's sharp return just inside the sideline. "Okay, I won, but—then what? How many cases has Herb Myerson won?"

Wrigley flinched visibly at the casual mention

of Mr. Myerson's name. It was like invoking a dark and powerful god. Wrigley was in awe of Miles, but he was afraid of Herb Myerson. There were rumors about the old man that came from an extremely reliable source—high-priced hookers.

"The old man?" Wrigley said innocently. "He's won more than anybody. He's a legend."

"And look at him," Miles said as if Wrigley had proved his point. "Eighty-seven years old, still the first one into the office every day; no home life . . ."

"Who needs a home when you've got a colostomy bag," Wrigley quipped, forgetting himself. Then he remembered and glanced around to make sure no one overhead.

"No wife, no family . . ." Miles short-hopped Niki's drop shot and flicked it over her head. "Wrigley—she can't really love this dope, can she?"

The question almost rocked Wrigley off his high perch. The invincible Miles Massey worried about romance. "Who? Who loves who?"

Niki wondered the same thing as she smacked a forehand straight at his crotch. Miles neatly blocked it and the ball popped over the net.

"Marilyn Rexroth signed a prenup with an oil millionaire."

The words reverberated in the brief quiet as Niki flung herself forward.

"A Massey prenup?" Wrigley's reply was punctuated by Niki's cry as she hit the ball, then hit the ground.

"Yeah."

As he scrambled after Niki's return, Wrigley realized two things. Marilyn Rexroth must be in love with the dope. And Miles just might be interested in Marilyn.

" 'Only love is in mind when the Massey is signed,' " Wrigley quoted.

*"Arghh!"* With an animal groan that was part rage and all pain, Miles whacked the ball directly at Niki's throat, almost beheading her. She ducked back just in time, then looked up at Wrigley.

They exchanged a knowing glance. Miles Massey was more than professionally interested in Marilyn Rexroth.

Janice had never been prouder of—or more in love with—her boss, Miles Massey. And she had never been so worried about him.

A month ago Miles was on top of the world. Every lawyer, judge and paralegal knew about his unprecedented total victory for his client Rex Rexroth.

Even Mr. Myerson, the reclusive head of the firm, had poked his head out of the door of his darkened sanctum and uttered a ghastly cry of triumph.

True, a few employees mistook it for a death rattle at first, but further investigation showed it to be Herb Myerson's deepest, most sincere sign of respect. He had left his desk and staggered across the room, dragging his IV unit, to deliver a public tribute to his esteemed young partner.

Miles, too, seemed exhilarated by the victory. He went about his work with renewed energy and had redecorated his office. His calendar became crammed with cases and consultations as news of his prowess spread—and Janice fielded all requests. She juggled his schedule expertly, making sure Miles had enough time for lunch, workouts and R&R. She even handed his dating, skillfully weeding out the bitches and gold diggers.

*Women see certain things so much better than men,* Janice reflected, sorting through a pile of mail. Even smart, successful, handsome heartbreakers like Miles Massey.

However, it all started breaking down. At first Janice thought it was a mild postvictory depression. Miles would spend a lot of time in his office deep in thought, distracted, seemingly a bit bored. But Janice didn't really take it seriously, she had seen him go through short periods of disenchantment. After six years as Miles Massey's personal assistant, Janice knew every mood and nuance of her beloved boss.

Then *she* came to the office—the bitch of bitches.

*I should have sworn Miles was in Paris that day, instead of announcing her uninvited ass,* Janice thought ruefully. *Fool that I am.*

Marilyn Rexroth's visit proved to be devastating. When she and her goofy fiancé finally left the office, Miles was a changed man. Tense, depressed, anxious, disinterested in his work; all the symptoms of a man carrying a major torch. He had begun drinking wine spritzers in the afternoon.

Suddenly, Janice found something that cut her brooding short. A square, tasteful envelope addressed by hand, in tasteful ink. She didn't have to look at the return address to know who had sent it.

And what it contained.

*Ohmigod, poor, brave Miles,* Janice thought. For an instant she considering destroying the envelope.

The phone rang, preventing her from doing something foolish.

"Hi Janice, it's me, is he in?"

Normally Janice would have put Holly Holtz on hold. Despite the usual tight buns and perfect blonde face, Holly had a tendency to whine and was pure gold digger. But Miles desperately needed human contact, especially today. And Holly could be a double espresso for his libido.

"Holly Holtz," she said cheerfully, when Miles answered the phone. She tried to make it sound like a special event.

"Can't talk now," Miles barked. "No more calls."

"Sorry Holly, he's in a meeting," Janice said regretfully. This time she meant it.

Janice sighed, hefting the wedding invitation from Marilyn Rexroth. *Well, I may as well deliver the bad news,* she thought, half rising. Then she sat right down.

*What, am I crazy?* Janice wondered, signaling the mailboy to her desk. *They kill the messenger around here.*

Walter the mailboy leered at her. "What's up?"

Janice handed him the wedding invitation. "Take this into Mr. Massey. It's urgent."

Walter's pimply leer was replaced by suspicion. He looked from the envelope to the door and back to the envelope. Then he looked at Janice to make sure he heard correctly.

"Now, Walter," Janice said firmly.

As Walter trudged the few feet to Miles's office, he squinted at the envelope he carried in both hands, as if it contained a bomb.

And it did.


Father Scott had begun his spiritual journey as a folk rock musician.

His band the Jack City Pilgrims cut one album and toured the small clubs for two years before Scott Earp hung up his fringed jacket for a white collar.

Father Scott had a vision for his ministry. He once sang his own musical version of The Lord's Prayer that began, "Our Father, who art in heaven, Hollywood be thy name . . ."

Although some believed his enthusiasm bordered on blasphemy, most were moved by Father Scott's message: God is love—not lust. God is forgiveness—not revenge. God is in all things large and small. For this he was regarded as eccentric. Which was perfect for Los Angeles.

So he established the First Church of the Living Swing—a ministry dedicated to worshiping the Lord through music. Be it hymns, psalms, prayers or sermons, Father Scott tried to say it with song.

Within a few years Father Scott had accumulated enough tax-free donations to build a gated five-unit compound on Franklin, a block from the Scientology Celebrity Centre. The compound was composed of five two-story stucco buildings painted in bright pastel shades from yellow to pink.

The pink building was the wedding chapel and Father Scott's special pride. He loved weddings.

To that end, he had equipped the chapel with a high-end sound system that could deliver special effects, and a battery of video cameras that could shoot the ceremony from any angle. Father Scott liked to call it "a full-service wedding service."

Actually, Father Scott's ace in the hole was parking. His facility could accommodate over a hundred and fifty vehicles. He booked at least ten weddings a week, stacking them between morning and afternoon.

The profits were astounding.

His accountants urged him to convert a second wedding chapel but they didn't get it.

Father Scott *was* the ceremony.

His music, his production and his performance created the vessel for God's love to bless a young couple's union.

*Of course, today's union was hardly young,* Father

Scott thought as he prepared himself for the ceremony. The bride was about twenty-eight and the groom was long past forty, but it would be a hell of a performance.

He checked his makeup, nothing elaborate, a light tan base and eyeliner, gave his hair a final spray and picked up his guitar.

*Showtime.*

He hit the monitor that dimmed the house lights and turned up the spots, then hit the **sound** monitor. As the canned background music began to rise, Father Scott strummed his guitar and began to sing:

*Parsley, sage, rosemary and thyme,*
*Remember me to one who lives there . . .*

Miles was about to have the mother of all nervous breakdowns.

*I knew I shouldn't have come,* he silently ranted. *How could she love a dope like Doyle?*

The crowd of beautiful, well-dressed people seemed to mock his question. For they were all there as witnesses to Marilyn's love for Howard D. Doyle.

*I knew I shouldn't have come,* Miles repeated like a mantra. His fabled serenity was lost, shredded by his emotions. *I'm lost,* he thought as the lights dimmed. He heard the chords of a guitar and a disembodied voice began to sing,

*Parsley, sage, rosemary and thyme,*
*Remember me to one who lives there . . .*

A portly man wearing a white spangled suit reminiscent of a Vegas performer strolled into view. As he continued to sing, a velvet curtain slid back revealing the bride and groom.

Marilyn was radiant in a white beaded silk dress that flattered her long, graceful neck and smooth shoulders. Standing at the altar she looked like a Renaissance Madonna.

The man standing next to her in a white suit and cowboy hat looked ridiculous.

*She once was a true love of mine . . .*

The song trailed off amid violins and the twittering of invisible birds. There was a low, appreciative murmur as everyone sat down.

Miles glanced at Wrigley and saw that his young associate was weeping softly. "What the hell is wrong with you?" Miles hissed, unable to conceal his irritation.

"I can't help it," Wrigley sniffled. "Even with the business we're in. I . . . it gets me every time."

"Is she going through with this, Wrigley?" Miles demanded, looking around angrily. "I can't believe she loves this stiff. I can't believe she's going through with it. Is she going through with this?"

"If she's not going through with it, she's cutting it awfully close," Wrigley murmured, dabbing his eyes.

As the crowd quieted for the exchange of vows, Miles considered storming the altar and carrying Marilyn away. He stared at Doyle with a mixture of disgust and horror. The white cowboy hat was a vile fashion statement. It screamed infantile asshole. It was like Gabby Hayes marrying Mona Lisa.

"Good morning, dear souls of God, I'm Father Scott," said the man in the spangled white suit. "Thank you all for coming to this celebration of the love between our two friends, Marilyn and Howard."

Beaming, Father Scott inclined his head to each of them and lightly strummed his guitar. Miles felt his stomach turn.

"Marilyn, Howard, you are about to embark on a great journey, a journey of love and caring and joy."

His pudgy smile turned somber and he strummed a low chord. "In today's cynical world it's so hard to take that great leap of faith aboard the ship of love and caring."

Father Scott strummed a few bell-like chords. With each note, Miles felt the pressure inside his skull increase. The minister went on.

"Today Marilyn and Howard are taking that leap and telling us, their friends, that they really do believe, that they do have faith, that they do love. They stand on the poop deck that is commitment." Father Scott struck a triumphant chord. "Next to the taffrail that is understanding." Another chord and his voice rose. "By the bo'sun who is . . . uh, also at the taffrail. And they are waving to us. Are they waving bon voyage?" He paused dramatically and lowered his voice.

"Or are they bidding us to follow, in our own vessels of love, joy and caring?" He strummed a crescendo. "Think about it."

The silence was broken only by the twittering of birds and Wrigley's snuffling. Father Scott raised his arms, revealing spangled sweat stains.

"Do you, Howard Drexler Doyle, take Marilyn to be your shipmate on this voyage through life, through gale and doldrum, seas choppy wild and calm?"

*The boob should have worn a sailor suit instead of that preposterous cowboy hat*, Miles railed silently. *It's like the good ship Lollipop. Any second now she's going to wake up and run. How could she love a dope like Doyle?*

"I do," Doyle said.

"And do you, Marilyn Rexroth, take Howard as your shipmate and companion, be it in first class or in steerage, to ports of every clime?"

*This is it,* Miles told himself. *This is where Sleeping Beauty wakes up. This is where she comes to and flies away from the big bad boob.*

"I do," Marilyn said.

"Argh!" Without warning, the pressure inside his skull blew. Wrigley stopped sniffling and some other heads turned. Miles bit his fist. Birds began to twitter.

"Then, by the power vested in me by the state of California, I now pronounce you man and wife."

Violins began to play, the audience applauded and Wrigley burst into tears. Miles also felt like crying. *I blew it,* he thought dismally. *Marilyn Rexroth is now Mrs. Boob. And there is absolutely nothing I can do about it.*

The reception was a lavish affair, held on the grounds of the Beverly Hills Hotel. One table held a large bride and groom made of sushi. Champagne flowed and the guests mingled like exotic birds, preening and chattering.

Father Scott had brought his guitar and he strolled about singing,

*I am just a poor boy,*
*Though my story's seldom told,*
*I have squandered my existence . . .*

*That's my sad story,* Miles brooded darkly. *I've squandered my existence.* He sighed and downed his champagne.

"What do you think?" Wrigley asked.

Miles looked down at the blue Tiffany box in his hand. Wrigley lifted the lid. Inside were twelve silver utensils that resembled the coffee stirrers at McDonald's.

"What are they?"

"Berry spoons," Wrigley said as if it was obvious.

Miles was unimpressed. "Spoons."

"*Berry* spoons," Wrigley corrected. "Everybody has spoons."

"And nobody *needs* berry spoons."

Wrigley clenched his teeth. "People. Eat. Berries."

Unable to contain the relentless pressure that had been escalating since Marilyn's first visit, Miles lashed out. "That's a cynical point of view. Where did you see these things anyway, in a

Martha Stewart catalogue? Next to the silver napkin rings? The stadium-seat ass warmers? Good God, Wrigley, how many kitschy-cutie material possessions do we have to amass—"

Wrigley cut him off. "Miles—why so angry?" he asked with a trace of genuine concern.

Before Miles could reply he was interrupted by the *ding, ding* of metal on glass. He looked up and saw Howard D. tapping a large bowie knife against a champagne flute.

*A bowie knife? How could she love this cretin?*

"Ladies and gentlemen, boys and girls," Howard rasped genially. "I know it's not common practice for the groom to give his bride a gift on their weddin' day. But folks, ever since I met Marilyn I just can't seem to stop givin' her things—" He smiled adoringly at Marilyn, who was seated beside him at the table.

There was a smattering of polite applause.

"—And I don't want to stop!"

This encouraged even more applause.

" 'Cause it feels durn good!"

Surprised laughter rippled across the party.

Miles gaped with a mixture of dismay and disbelief. *She loves this boob of the month?*

Howard turned and took one of Marilyn's hands between his big paws. She beamed up at him as if viewing the statue of David.

"Darlin', like the padre said, I want there to be love and trust between us, love and trust and nothin' else," Howard told her. "Now I'm not too big on words . . ." He winked at the gallery, who laughed appreciatively.

"Well, okay—I *am* big on words, but I'm also big on deeds. And thisa here deed is just to show you . . . oh, shucks, honey . . ."

With elaborate slowness, Howard reached into his breast pocket and extracted a piece of paper. "Bring out the barbecue sauce, Chow Sing!"

A Chinese gentleman wearing a chef's hat appeared, bearing a large plate and a bowl of barbecue sauce. He placed them in front of Doyle, who sat down and tied a napkin bib around his neck.

"This is for you, darlin'," he announced solemnly. Howard tore a strip from the document in his hand, dipped it in barbecue sauce and began to eat it. As he chewed, he tore off more strips until his mouth was stuffed with paper.

"Thish is for you, darlin' . . ." Howard repeated, lips smeared with dark red sauce.

Miles watched in stunned silence, unable to comprehend the meaning of Howard's incredibly gross display. The other guests seemed equally confused and began to murmur among themselves. The guests began nodding their heads and the murmur grew in volume, generating a smattering of applause, which escalated to small cheers, bravos, more applause and finally wild cheers of approval.

When it finally dawned on Miles, all his tension, anxiety, depression—the industrial-strength pressure—all of it instantly fled, like air from a balloon, leaving him giddy. *Bravo, baby,* he thought. *I couldn't have done better myself.*

Slowly, rhythmically, he thumped his hands together, flashing a victory grin. "Brilliant!" he called out. "Brilliant!"

Wrigley remained puzzled. Not only by Howard Doyle's strange act, but by the total transformation it had triggered in Miles. His expression of brooding anger had vanished, replaced by the glazed smile of a religious zealot.

"What is it, Miles?" Wrigley whined anxiously. "What is it?" He seemed to be the only one at the reception who didn't know.

Miles continued to applaud. "Brilliant! It's the prenup. It's the *Prenup!* BY GOD, IT'S BRILLIANT!"

Wrigley's eyes widened with comprehension. He looked over at Howard Doyle, who was still chewing a great wad of paper, barbecue sauce dribbling down his chin.

"This is for you, darlin' . . ." Howard kept saying between swallows.

Wrigley burst into tears. "That's . . . the most romantic thing . . . I've ever seen . . . in my *whole life!*" he blurted, sobbing wildly.

Miles wasn't even irritated by Wrigley's sentimental blubbering. *By God, she pulled it off,* he exulted, still applauding. *She my kind of woman. And she doesn't love that boob any more than I do.*

"THISH IS FOR YOU, DARLIN'!" Howard blared.

Miles waited until the crowd had thinned a bit before moving to the punch bowl where Marilyn stood, accepting congratulations. He felt like his old self—confident, optimistic, inspired. Never, never in his career had he witnessed a more magnificent coup. *Brilliantly bloodless,* he reflected as he approached the lovely bride.

"I'd like to offer my congratulations," he said, looking deeply into her dark eyes. "That was a beautiful gesture of Howard's."

"Howard is a beautiful person—a diamond in the rough," she added with a mischievous twinkle.

He leaned closer. "And I have a feeling that

someday soon you're going to take the diamond and leave the rough."

A sly smile crossed her sensual lips. "In a month or two. As soon as I've established that I tried to make the marriage work."

Miles leaned even closer. "May I offer my services?"

She shrugged and looked away. "Thanks, but I'm going to retain Freddy Bender. Poor Freddy, he was so blue after my last divorce."

While stung, Miles tried to accept gracefully. "I admire your loyalty—to lawyers. I guess without the prenup this will be something even Freddy can manage." Miles lowered his voice. "But how did you get Howard to do it? It seemed like he thought it was his idea."

Her face lit up like an Oscar winner, part triumph and part professional pride. "Oh, Mr. Massey," she teased. "Surely you've addressed enough juries to appreciate the power of suggestion."

*I definitely appreciate you*, Miles thought. "Mnn, look—now that your marriage is winding down—have dinner with me," he suggested casually.

"Oh no," Marilyn snapped. "Nothing doing until the ink is dry on the settlement."

Miles gave her an indulgent smile, like an

uncle bestowing a blessing on his favorite niece. "This will be no settlement," he told her. "If I know Marilyn Rexroth, this will be total and complete annihilation."

As if in cosmic accord, a rumble of distant thunder punctuated his words.

# CHAPTER
# TWELVE

**R**ex Rexroth was having the party of his life. He was about to be the first railroad stud to join the Mile High Club. And his crew Bambi and Patti were going to help him achieve this momentous landmark—or more properly—this skymark.

Since the real estate deal came together, Rex had become richer than he had ever imagined. With the money came freedom to explore the possibilities, the parameters—the nooks and crannies—of his sexuality. No longer afraid of being outed, no longer embarrassed to express himself fully as a steaming, steel-driving train stud.

*And Miles Massey made it possible,* Rex noted dreamily as he surveyed the refurbished cabin of his new Learjet. It looked like the inside of an old-fashioned train station. But the best part was the heavy-gauge track running around the floor of the cabin.

Sitting on the track was a miniature locomotive with a caboose attached. And sitting on the locomotive, wearing nothing but his railroad shorts, a striped railroad cap and a red bandanna, was Rex himself—being pushed along by his naked crew women.

Up front, in the cockpit, the pilot listened to Rex's cavorting over his headset. Captain Greg Granger was a Mormon and could handle the concept of polygamy, but this was way beyond multiple females. His new boss had hit a new low in freaky behavior.

After a few more minutes of listening, Greg shook his head.

"Jesus . . ." was all he could say.

His co-pilot Colby Dirk glanced at him. "What?"

"I've heard . . ." Greg took a deep breath. "I've heard some sick things on my . . ."

"What?" Colby urged.

Greg reached up and threw a small toggle switch. Abruptly the droning silence in the cockpit was awash with the sound of screaming, laughter and music.

*Oh, Casey Jones was the rounder's name,*
*T'was on the 6:02 that he rode to fame . . .*

"You're ridin' to fame, big boy," screamed a female voice.

"Give him a full head of steam," a second female giggled. "He's goin' for the world record!"

"Caboose! Caboose!" the first female shouted.

The two pilots exchanged a puzzled glance. They had flown a fair share of raunchy executives. But nothing like this. *What the hell could our new boss be doing back there?* Colby wondered. He would have to install a video camera.

Back in the main cabin, Bambi and Patti, naked except for their train conductor caps, were pushing Rex's locomotive around the track, pausing every few feet to stoke his furnace.

At the same time Rex kept singing railroad songs, drunk with his new freedom.

Listening in the cockpit, the co-pilot was awestruck.

"Who is this guy?"

"Rex Rexroth, the minimall king," the pilot said grimly. "Getting to be the richest man on the West Coast, from what they say."

Colby shook his head. "Jesus."

They both knew what he meant. Another two-ton gorilla to baby-sit.

From the speakers came Rex's voice:

*Come all ye rounders, if you wanna hear . . .*

The co-pilot suddenly remembered something.

"Why're we going to Muncie?"

The pilot shrugged. "He's thinking of buying Indiana."

He pulled back the throttle and the jet soared higher above the vast ocean of clouds.

*What a difference a day makes,* Janice reflected happily, as she made the arrangements for Miles's star speaking engagement in Vegas.

Her boss had returned from the Rexroth wedding a renewed man. Miles had redoubled his workload and was making plans to redecorate his office. *Always a good sign,* Janice noted. And always fun when *World of Interiors* magazine came to photograph. In one spread they included a shot of Janice. It hung framed on her bathroom wall.

Janice made sure Miles's suite at Caesars Palace was big without being gaudy. One year they booked him in a honeymoon suite by mistake and Miles had to sleep in a heart-shaped bed with pink sheets. He claimed the sheets kept him awake all night.

Janice knew better. What kept him up all night was Holly Holtz, who had been stalking Miles for months and cornered him in Vegas. *The slut,* Janice observed without emotion. She couldn't blame Holly. Lots of women stalked Miles, and lots of them succeeded.

*Which technically makes him a slut,* Janice mused, putting his schedule, tickets and reservations in a red folder.

However, it made no difference. In Vegas, everyone was a slut.

Caesars Palace stood as a crown jewel in the dazzling tiara of spectacular structures known as the Las Vegas strip.

Adorning its glamorous façade was an alabaster replica of the statue of David—classically proportioned torso, muscular shoulders, strong, graceful neck. That same divine David sculpted by Michelangelo, which graced the main square in Florence, Italy.

Except the David at Caesars Palace was three times the size. Its massive head loomed above the parking lot, staring out into the darkness with brooding nobility. Far below, a marquee announced the hotel's special events. Tonight it read:

Miles usually enjoyed Vegas. He was right at home with its unabashed pursuit of pleasure. But tonight, as he strolled briskly through Caesars' casino, dropping coins in each slot machine he passed, Miles was aware of a strange, alien emotion. He felt lonely.

Granted, he wasn't alone. Wrigley was right behind him with a bucket to scoop up his winnings. And Miles won on every pull. Each successive machine clattered with the sound of pouring coins as it paid off.

It annoyed Wrigley to no end.

"You know why I can't stand Las Vegas, Wrigley?" Miles asked over his shoulder.

"Why is that?" Wrigley said dutifully. Actually he always thought Miles liked the place. He certainly won enough money.

"The emptiness. The isolation. The dacronization of the moral fabric." Miles pulled the slot machine handle. "Do *you* know what I mean?"

"Oh sure," Wrigley said, as coins rained into the cup. "The dangling conversations, the superficial sighs." He scooped most of the coins into the nearly full bucket. He put the leftovers in his pocket, for later.

Miles moved to the next area. "You tell me, Wrigley: Has Las Vegas democratized marriage—or cheapened it?" He paused and glanced back at the bucket.

Wrigley froze, then sheepishly took the few quarters from his pocket and added them to the pile in the bucket.

Miles kept walking. "You see, Wrigley, people get to Vegas and all of a sudden the rules of the moral universe don't apply. If God is dead, all things are possible."

He stopped at a slot machine and pulled the handle. Coins filled the cup. "Why, I saw an ad in the paper here—'No-Fault Divorce'—two-week divorce without a lawyer."

Miles glared at Wrigley indignantly. "It made me sick to my stomach. *No-fault* divorce? Good God, talk about an oxymoron. What's the world coming to?"

Wrigley tried to calm him down. Miles was always hyper before one of these things. "One man can only do so much," he offered.

Miles whirled, scowling in irritation. "What the hell are you talking about?" he demanded.

Wrigley swallowed hard. Wrong approach.

Abruptly Miles's eyebrows shot up and a gleaming smile wiped off the scowl. "Freddy!" he shouted with a mixture of surprise and unexpected enthusiasm.

Wrigley turned. There indeed was Freddy Bender, crossing the floor to the elevators. "I had lunch with Freddy Bender yesterday," he confided. "He tells me that Marilyn Rexroth-Doyle is now richer than Croesus."

Wrigley didn't mention that Freddy tried to hire him away from Miles.

Miles continued to smile in Freddy's direction. "Ah, but is she richer than *Mrs*. Croesus?"

He made it sound like a Zen koan.

Wrigley took the low road. His repressed resentment spilled over. It wasn't easy being the associate of a man who always won. "She could buy and sell you ten times over," he taunted.

But Miles wasn't listening.

His gaze, his attention, his entire being was focused on a lithe female crossing the gaming floor. "My God—" he muttered, as if he'd sighted Atlantis. "Is that her?"

Wrigley looked. Her face was partially obscured by dark glasses, but her regal walk and chic Alexander McQueen outfit hinted that it was Marilyn Rexroth-Doyle. She was leading an impeccably groomed Afghan hound, who appeared to be of show quality. Both mistress and hound strode with heads high through the discordant noise and tawdry lights of the casino until they joined Freddy Bender at the elevator.

"Mnn, Freddy said she'd be flying in with him," Wrigley said cautiously. "Celebrating, I guess."

To Wrigley's surprise Miles remained unruffled. "I'm fascinated by that creature," he confessed, staring in rapture. "She deserves every penny. They pay great athletes a king's ransom—well, Wrigley look at *her*—an athlete at the peak of her powers."

Miles snatched the bucket from Wrigley, spilling a layer of quarters.

"Excuse me," he grunted, trotting off toward the elevators.

*Uh-oh,* Wrigley thought. *It's about to happen again. For some reason his brains turn to blubber when Marilyn is in the house.*

"Miles, you stay away from her," Wrigley called after him. "Take a cold shower and recite your keynote address."

Miles didn't hear.

Wrigley heaved a sigh and picked up the quarters he'd spilled. It was only the biggest speech of his distinguished professional career, Wrigley fumed, hunting down the stray coins. All

Miles needed was for Marilyn Rexroth-Doyle to puncture his macho balloon and send him into another tailspin.

Wrigley moved to a nearby slot machine and absently fed it five coins. He pulled the handle and glanced over at the elevators. Miles had nearly caught up to Marilyn and her Afghan.

An alarm went off. Wrigley blinked and looked at the machine. Three cherries were lined up neatly in front of him. Dazed, he listened to the merry clatter of coins sliding into the cup.

*I won,* he thought incredulously. *Miles's quarters brought me luck. Maybe it's time I stopped worrying about my boss,* Wrigley decided, watching him slip into the elevator with Marilyn just before the doors closed. *Even when he's making a fool of himself, Miles does better than ninety-nine percent of the world.*

# CHAPTER
# THIRTEEN

Miles hadn't felt this way about anyone since high school.

It wasn't just that she was sensual and smart, she had real spirit. *She could use a tad more humor,* Miles reflected, hurrying to the elevator. *Marilyn can be chilly—grim, in fact.*

He slipped between the closing doors, nudging the Afghan aside. Marilyn looked annoyed until she saw who it was. Then she merely looked chilly. She acknowledged him with a cool smile, as if uncertain where she had seen him before.

"You're looking well, Marilyn," Miles congratulated. "Obscene wealth becomes you."

She took off her dark glasses. "Oh, hello,

Miles. I guess I should have known you'd be here." She made it sound as if he was there to steal wallets.

"Be here?" He flashed a modest grin. "I'm the keynote speaker."

He may as well have said he was the night manager at Burger King. She accepted the news with a disdainful shrug. "How nice for you."

"Whose Community Property Is It Anyway? Nailing Your Spouse's Assets," he said proudly.

"Excuse me?" She looked at him as if about to call security.

"My speech."

She checked the floor indicator. "I'm sure it will bring the house down."

Miles recovered his composure. "It's an easy crowd. At this point, you're probably the only person I can't teach anything to."

"Mnnn." There was an uncomfortable pause.

Miles jumped right in. "Correct me, but— since by now the ink must be dry—I believe I have the right to collect."

Marilyn seemed confused. "Oh . . . ?"

"You promised to have dinner with me once you were free."

Her smile was playful. Miles had learned to beware of that smile.

"I said I wouldn't, while I wasn't, which

implies no promise once I am," she declared breezily.

Of course, she was right on each point. "Noted," Miles conceded, leaning closer. "Let me rephrase . . ." Absently he reached down to pet the Afghan. "I would be delighted, honored even, if you would—AIEEEAHHH!"

They both looked down. The Afghan had Miles's hand placidly clamped in its mouth.

"Howard," Marilyn scolded. "Bad boy!"

The dog placidly dropped Miles's hand. Miles wondered if the Afghan was on Prozac.

"Cute," he muttered, rubbing the teeth marks denting his skin. "Named after your ex?"

Marilyn shrugged. "I'm sentimental."

The elevator's *ding* announced her floor.

Marilyn's expression softened a notch. "Well, I have no plans this evening," she said, stepping into the hall. "I suppose a little dinner couldn't do any harm."

Miles grinned. "Franco's at eight."

He was still grinning when the doors closed.

Marilyn allowed herself a small playful smile. Phase Two of her master plan was well under way . . .

Marilyn was aware of the heads turning in her direction as she crossed the casino floor on her way to meet Miles for dinner. But her mind was focused on the task ahead. She had been anticipating this for a long time.

The constant whir and clack of the machines, the cries of the winners, the electric hum of money and excitement were lost on her, as were the admiring stares. She had dressed carefully, seductively, but not for pleasure. This night, Marilyn was on a deadly mission.

She had to admit Miles had chosen well.

Franco's restaurant was small by Vegas standards. Its intimate feel enhanced the delicious Italian cuisine. It also boasted a world-class wine list. Marilyn knew that reservations at Franco's were at a premium—however, she wasn't overly surprised to discover that Miles was a close personal friend of Franco himself.

It seems Miles had represented Franco during a messy divorce and managed to salvage his house and his restaurant. For which Franco was eternally grateful. In fact, after Miles made the introductions, Franco withdrew and sent a fabulous bottle of wine to their table.

The waiter didn't appear to notice the Afghan seated patiently beside Marilyn. "Veuve Clicquot Ponsardin 1982," he announced, proffering the bottle.

Miles waited until it was uncorked, then took

the bottle from the waiter. "Thank you. I'll do the rest," he said smoothly.

As the waiter departed, Miles filled Marilyn's goblet and his own.

"You know, Marilyn," he said softly, "this is a moment to savor. Once we were adversaries, but we're also professionals. Let's raise a glass in friendship."

*Like Julius Caesar and his good friend Brutus,* Marilyn thought, raising her glass.

"To victory," she offered. And she meant it.

Miles sipped his wine. "So how does it feel?"

Marilyn cocked an inquiring eye. Miles elaborated.

"Victory? Independence?"

"Ah, yes." Marilyn looked down at her drink. "Well, frankly, Miles . . ."

"Mnn, not everything you'd hoped for, huh?" Miles said, voice dripping with empathy. "I know the feeling,"

*I'll bet you do,* Marilyn thought, but she noticed how handsome he looked in candlelight. For a moment she felt a pang of guilt. Then it passed.

"Independence is a two-edged sword," she sighed. "A friend of mine—my best friend, Sarah Sorkin?" She waited for him to react. He shrugged.

"Sarah Battista O'Flanagan Sorkin?"

Miles brightened. "The O'Flanagan settlement, of course." He remembered it well. Despite the fact that Sarah Battista O'Flanagan had been caught in the garage with her gardener, and that her first marriage had ended for the same reason—with the same gardener—Miles had engineered a huge settlement on her behalf. "Heh-heh," he gloated.

"Heh-heh-heh." Marilyn smiled appreciatively. "Anyway, three fine settlements, more money than she could ever hope to spend, her vaunted independence and . . ."

Miles held up his hand. "Yes. Don't tell me. She sits around the house afraid to see people. Afraid to put her portfolio into play."

"And only a peptic ulcer to keep her warm at night." As Marilyn sipped her wine she realized how wise Miles was, as well as very sexy.

Miles heaved a long sigh. "Mnn, yes. At a certain point you achieve your goals and—"

"—Find out you're still not satisfied," she finished.

Miles looked at her, his expression one of surprise, wonder and a certain respect. "Mnn. Well—shall we order?"

Marilyn felt a twinge of disappointment. She had been waiting for him to kiss her. "Yes, I—well, I'm not really . . ."

"Not hungry, huh?" Miles smiled. "Neither am I," he confided, voice low and husky.

His eyes found hers, and for a long, pensive moment they gazed at each other in the flickering candlelight. Miles reached out and took her hand. When his fingers touched her skin, Marilyn felt a tiny shock of recognition.

They left the restaurant hand in hand, oblivious to the constant activity in the casino, oblivious to everything except each other. Marilyn kept her grip on Howard's leash, but her resolve was slipping. *Don't go soft now that you've come so far,* Marilyn urged silently. *Just because he's handsome, witty, sensitive and sexy . . . that's no reason, is it?*

Standing side by side in the elevator, Marilyn was acutely aware of the animal energy between them. So was Howard, who crouched down and keened softly.

When the elevator reached the twenty-sixth floor, they both got out and stood in the flocked hallway, looking at each other. Miles leaned closer and she could feel his warm breath on her lips.

"Marilyn," he whispered.

Gently she put her finger on his mouth. Sadly, he pulled back and relinquished her hand. Although they hadn't kissed, it felt as if they had.

They both knew it. Before she did something rash, Marilyn turned and walked quickly to her suite.

Miles watched her go with a mixture of regret and optimism. *One base down,* he speculated happily. *Three to go.*

Marilyn was playing another game entirely. *Three bases down,* she noted. *One to go.*

She steeled herself for the nasty task ahead. The part where she chopped off his head, and his balls.

# CHAPTER
# FOURTEEN

A clap of thunder shook the rolling darkness. It echoed madly against distant walls. Lightning flickered, illuminating a figure shifting in the gloom. A hunched figure pointed a cadaverous, liver-spotted hand with an IV tube trailing down like an alien snake.

Then he lifted his head, revealing a mummy-gray face, seamed with corruption and hollowed with unhappiness. When the figure spoke, his voice was a rasping hiss. "Eighteen hunnut billable hours, twelve hunnut 'n twenty-one motions tuh void . . ."

Wailing cries rose up as the voice continued to drone.

". . . five hunnut 'n sixty-faw summary judgments. . . . A hunnut twenty-nine t'ousand, four hunnut 'n seventeen lunches chahged . . ."

Somewhere a phone was ringing. It rang again louder, louder, until . . .

Miles sat bolt upright, skin glistening with cold sweat.

The phone beside his bed was ringing. *I've been having a nightmare,* Miles realized with mild relief. He took a deep breath and picked up the phone.

"Hello?"

"Miles?"

He recognized Marilyn's breathy voice. But it had a strange edge.

"Hello, Marilyn?"

"Sarah Sorkin just died."

The four words skidded across his brain like tires on ice and crashed against his skull. Through the smoke and silence, Miles managed to collect himself.

"Wait there," he said hoarsely.

As he rolled out of bed, Miles's brain was still trying to fit where he'd just been—into what he'd just heard. *That dream,* he had been having the same dream for weeks and he had the distinct impression it was a warning. Like the Ghosts of Christmas Past, Present and Watch Your Ass.

*Poor Sarah, she had everything to live for: beauti-*

*ful, rich, young,* Miles thought. *But she died alone— of fear. Fear of losing some money, fear of making a mistake, fear of falling in love . . .*

*Just like me,* Miles realized, heading for the door.

Less than five minutes later, Miles burst into Marilyn's suite, a Caesars Palace robe covering his blue pajamas. Marilyn was stretched on the couch, also wearing a Caesars robe. She was weeping uncontrollably. Howard the Afghan rested his head dolefully on her lap.

*The nightmare was a sign,* Miles thought feverishly. He moved to the couch and nudged the Afghan aside.

"Marilyn," he murmured, embracing her. Her body was a perfect fit in his arms.

"Her ulcer . . ." Marilyn sobbed, ". . . perforated . . . infection."

"There, there," was all he could say. But his mind and emotions were in a mad dash up reality hill and his emotions were way out front. He knew that he and Marilyn were made for each other, belonged together.

This tragedy had wounded her to the core. And it had wounded him, as well. "There, there . . ." he repeated softly.

"Peritonitis . . . Miles . . ."

When she spoke his name it went right

through him. "What, Marilyn?" he whispered, aware of the heat generated by their closeness. It radiated deep into his bone and flesh, charging his spine until it glowed like a fluorescent tube.

"She was alone." Marilyn's voice cracked. "She'd been dead . . . two days until . . ." Her body pressed against his as she struggled for breath. ". . . until her pilates instructor found her!" Her voice was washed away by a fresh wave of sobs.

Miles felt his heart pounding against his ribs. *Sarah died of loneliness,* he thought. If she hadn't been alone, someone could have gotten her help. If she hadn't been alone, she'd be alive now.

"Oh, Miles." Again, he felt a twinge when she whispered his name. As he continued rocking her like a child, he had a vision of Marilyn alone and helpless in a remote ski chalet, Marilyn floating facedown in a pool, Marilyn falling down stairs; a gamut of gut-wrenching scenarios.

*What kind of man am I?* he brooded. *A silly man? Or someone who wants to create something meaningful, to make a difference. It's time to step up and take charge—it's time to build a life with the woman I love. Or that nightmare will be me.*

"Marilyn, listen to me," he said, face grim. He took her shoulders and gazed into her tear-swollen eyes. She never looked so vulnerable, or so beautiful. As he stared, he could tell she understood.

"No arguments," Miles said huskily. "No discussions. I'll have Wrigley meet us at the Wee Kirk o' the Heather!"

For a long, tender moment Marilyn stopped sobbing and looked at him, her face shining with joy.

It was one of the top ten moments in Miles's life.

Mr. McKinnon had never been to Scotland. The closest he'd ever been to Europe was Pennsylvania.

The Scottish-theme wedding chapel was his son and daughter-in-law's bright idea. They had visited Great Britain on their honeymoon and decided the Scottish thing would make a good investment.

And McKinnon had to agree the place made good, steady money. The additional income from renting kilts, tam-o'-shanters and shawls was even better. Then there were the souvenirs like the tartan wedding albums and his favorite, the plaid garters.

The best part was it kept his wife occupied. All her life she had wanted to be a performer on stage and the wedding chapel gave her the opportunity.

As for McKinnon, he liked to run a tight ship, and these last-minute romantic fools were late. Time was money. Which would be shown in their bill, payable by cash or credit card, no checks, please.

McKinnon could see a male party with a brief-case waiting outside. If it was the groom, he was already in trouble. If it wasn't the groom, he'd better move along before McKinnon called the cops.

He ran a tight ship, right out to the sidewalk, where the tartan plaid neon sign read WEE KIRK O' THE HEATHER.

Unaware that he was being closely observed, Wrigley waited impatiently for Miles to arrive. In the years he had been with Miles, this was the most outrageously incredible caper he had ever assisted.

Wrigley wasn't sure Miles was doing the right thing.

He'd never known Miles to be so impetuous when it came to major decisions. Marilyn Rexroth had just divorced Howard Doyle and was swimming in oil money, and yet—Miles had called for a Massey prenup.

Wrigley hefted his briefcase and checked his gold Rolex.

It could be a brilliant ploy. Miles never did

anything without a good reason. But this . . . Wrigley felt his eyes welling up . . . this was so romantic.

After a few minutes a cab pulled up to the curb where Wrigley was pacing impatiently. Marilyn emerged, mascara slightly smudged. Miles followed, chin set with determination. Both were identically clad in Caesars Palace bathrobes.

"Wrigley," Miles said, his voice thick with emotion. "My friend."

He clapped Wrigley's shoulders, then put a protective arm around Marilyn and started walking to the entrance.

Wrigley sprang into action. He reached into his briefcase and pulled out a thin sheaf of papers and a CD. "The marriage vows are from an old Arapaho dawn-greeting ceremony. The music is Simon and Garfunkel. And this . . ." He pulled out a single sheet of legal paper. ". . . is the Massey prenup."

Marilyn looked at Miles, who smiled reassuringly. "Don't worry, dearest, I'll take care of everything."

A white-haired man wearing a yellow plaid tam and a flinty expression watched them enter and approach the reception desk. He pressed both hands on the counter and leaned forward like a pugnacious old pit bull.

"You the two gettin' married?" he barked, eyeing their bathrobes suspiciously.

Miles looked at Wrigley, who leaned closer and whispered in his ear, "Mr. McKinnon will be officiating. Sorry . . . short notice, that kind of thing."

"Pen," Miles snapped.

Wrigley hastily pulled a ballpoint from his breast pocket and clicked it. Miles snatched the pen and the prenup. As he turned to Marilyn his tone and manner softened.

"Darling, you're welcome to examine this. It's the Massey prenup, which, as you well know, is iron-clad—"

"I tried to reach Freddy Bender—" Wrigley put in, as if to explain.

Miles nodded. "We tried to reach Freddy Bender to have him here for your protection, as well—"

"Couldn't get him," Wrigley added, smiling at Marilyn.

"—But we couldn't get him," Miles affirmed.

Mr. McKinnon slapped his hands on the counter. He had already missed *The Sopranos*. "Are you here to get married or to bullshit?!"

Miles glared at the old man. *Where did Wrigley find this insensitive old crocodile?* "Sir!" he warned. "Please!"

He turned and saw that Marilyn had taken out her reading glasses and was scanning the prenup. She murmered aloud as she read. "If for any reason . . . dissolution . . . party of the first part . . . all right."

Without ceremony Marilyn took the pen and signed it. She looked at Miles questioningly. "Now you can't hope to benefit from the marriage."

"Not in any way," Miles told her solemnly.

"My wealth is completely protected?"

"As if a lead veil had been drawn across it."

"And you still want to marry me?" she asked softly.

Miles drew her close. "More than ever."

Wrigley couldn't help it. He looked from Miles to Marilyn and burst into tears. It was all so . . . romantic. His boss, the great attorney Miles Massey, was also a great lover in the classic sense; like Cyrano, Dante, Sinatra. . . .

"Well then, children!" Mr. McKinnon rubbed his hands together and surveyed their Caesars Palace robes.

"Will ye be rentin' kilts?"

Miles chose the men's outfits.

Both he and Wrigley were dressed in blue blazers and kilts as they waited at the altar.

Marilyn appeared wearing a jaunty tam and a tartan shawl. She looked radiant as she moved beside Miles.

Behind them a blue-haired organist played a leisurely version of "Hawaiian War Chant." Mr. McKinnon seemed to have difficulty reading from his clipboard as he conducted the ceremony.

The Arapaho dawn-greeting ceremony gave him the most trouble, especially the chants in gratitude for the new day. In fact, Mr. McKinnon almost missed the whole point had not Wrigley stepped in. Through his tears he explained that this—their sacred union in matrimony—was the dawn of a new day, a new era. Sniffling, he began to chant,

*Mighty father sun,*
*Who gives his seed to Mother Earth, come,*
*Warm your waiting maiden . . .*

Mr. McKinnon squinted dourly, as if Wrigley were chanting Celtic insults and waited for his quavering voice to trail off.

However, when it came to familiar territory the old man warmed to his part. "Do you, uh . . ." he peered at the clipboard. "Miles Longfellow Massey of Massey, Myerson, Sloan and Gurolnick, LLP . . ." He looked at Miles disapprovingly. "Take Marilyn Hamilton Rexroth-Doyle to be your lawful wedded wife, to—"

"I do, yah," Miles said eagerly. "I do, uh-huh."

"Let me finish!" Mr. McKinnon barked. He fixed Miles with his flinty glare. "Jesus—have ya never been married before?"

Wrigley was amazed to see Miles actually chastened. He stared down like a little boy. Marilyn saw it, too, and her eyes grew misty.

". . . To have and to hold, to love and to cherish, till death do ye part?" the old man continued.

Everyone waited. Miles stared contritely at his shoes. Finally Marilyn nudged him.

Miles looked up. "I do."

"And do you Marilyn Hamilton Rexroth-Doyle, take Miles Longfellow Massey of Massey, Myerson, Sloan and Gurolnick LLP, to be your lawful wedded husband, to have and to hold, to love and cherish, till death do ye part?"

Marilyn gazed at Miles. At that moment she resembled a Renaissance Madonna wearing a tam. "I do," she said fervently.

Mr. McKinnon raised his arms. "I now pronounce ye man and wife." He dropped his arms and the dissonant wail of a swirl of bagpipes advanced toward the altar. An elderly blue-haired woman in tartan kilts and shawl slowly goose-stepped down the aisle, playing the bag-pipes as Miles kissed his new bride.

Overcome with emotion, Wrigley began blubbering.

Miles Massey, the top matrimonial attorney in America, was now a potential client. It was unbearably romantic. He wondered if *World of Interiors* would buy the magazine rights.

Miles had returned to the honeymoon suite. And this time he was looking forward to the red satin sheets keeping him awake.

Still wearing his kilt, Miles unlocked the door, then swept Marilyn up in his arms. Staggering slightly he carried her inside to the platform with the heart-shaped bed that looked out over the rainbow lights of the Las Vegas strip.

Miles looked deeply into Marilyn's eyes and kissed her. The sudden flare when their lips met cooled and she stiffened in his arms.

*She's been under a tremendous amount of stress,* Miles reminded. In his enthusiasm he'd forgotten how much Sarah's death had wounded her. And that was only a few hours ago. *Be very gentle,* he told himself.

"Marilyn?" he whispered. "Are you all right?"

"No. No," she said breathlessly, pulling free. "This is wrong."

He was confused. "Is it the kilt?"

"Miles—do you love me?"

The question surprised and thrilled him. He looked at her mischievous dark eyes, sensual lips and mysterious Mona Lisa smile. She was the female principal, Mother Earth, she was all women.

"More than anything," he said gravely.

"Can I trust you?"

He nodded. "You can trust me."

For a breathless moment she searched his face. Then she rolled over and groped for her purse. She fished out a folded sheet of legal paper, held it high and ripped it in half. With a playful smile she tossed both pieces in the air like confetti.

Miles watched in slack-jawed disbelief. *The Massey prenup!*

"Dear . . . you're exposed," he said, voice hushed.

"A siting duck . . ." A smoky curtain fell over her eyes and she leaned back against the red satin pillow.

Miles had enjoyed sex with many women but never before had he made love. Marilyn's body flowed in his arms as if she was part of him, every curve of her flesh fitting every hollow of his. When their lips met their souls linked in a slow, sensual ballet and they seemed weightless.

For hours they remained locked in their embrace, Marilyn's smooth skin slick with his sweat as the heat of their bodies lifted them higher. And while aloft on that cosmic flight of flesh and soul, Miles was transported, transformed and reborn.

The nightmares and the emptiness had been instantly vanquished, incinerated by the intensity of their love. And in the midst of the rapture generated by their intertwined limbs, their merging spirits, Miles saw his destiny clearly for the first time.

He had found true purpose for his life. To protect and cherish the future mother of his children, the cornerstone of his new family. And to found a dynasty based on love, trust and dignity: Massey, Massey & Massey LLP.

Outside, the lights of Las Vegas twinkled like stars in a freshly created universe.

# CHAPTER
# FIFTEEN

It was the culmination of a series of momentous transformations, each deeper than the last. Miles felt as if his very soul had been washed, bleached, spun dry and ironed. He'd been . . . redeemed. He'd been given a second chance to build a meaningful life.

"I won't be long," he promised, hurriedly putting on his rumpled jacket from last night's dinner. "But this needs to be done."

"I'll miss you, darling." Lying on the heart-shaped bed, Marilyn blew him a languid kiss as he strode out the door.

Miles didn't bother with a tie. In fact, he had skipped most of the amenities associated with an event of this import. His hair was rumpled, his face was unshaven and his eyes were baggy from twenty hours of champagne and love.

But his face had a glow, the inner fire of one who comes armed with the truth.

Miles marched across the casino, oblivious to the tawdry siren call of fast money and sex, straight to the heart of his mission. And when he arrived, they were all waiting for him.

The banquet hall was packed with attorneys from all over the world. And in their world, Miles Massey was king. Up on the podium Secretary Bombach spotted his entrance and banged his gavel for order.

Bombach had been eagerly anticipating Miles's arrival. Like many of the attorneys gathered there, he was in awe of the creator of the Massey prenup, of the man who pulled a client through a California divorce without paying one red cent and who was president of the powerful group assembled there today.

"I hereby declare the twelfth congress of the National Organization of Matrimonial Attorneys Nationwide . . . open!" Secretary Bombach called, slamming his gavel.

There was a general murmur from the large audience composed mostly of men in their forties, dressed in expensive Italian suits. By comparison Miles looked like a panhandler who had wandered in by mistake.

Bombach banged his gavel once more. "As our first order of business, it is my privilege to call to the podium our keynote speaker who is none other than the society's president! From the Los Angeles firm of Massey, Myerson, Sloan and Gurolnick, please welcome a man whose name is synonymous with bitter disputes and big awards—Miles Massey!"

Miles received genuinely warm applause as he made his way to the podium. Squinting, as if slightly dazed, he mounted the podium and shook the secretary's hand.

He turned to face the audience and fished a sheaf of papers from his inside pocket. "Thank you, Secretary Bombach," he began, voice tight and wooden. "And thank you, ladies and gentlemen."

Miles looked down at the papers in his hand. "In the world of . . ." He coughed, and looked around apologetically. He stared down at the speech as if seeing it for the first time. Then he tried again.

"In the world of matrimonial law there are multiple tactics . . ."

Miles couldn't go on. The words on the paper were meaningless now. His true message had been welling up inside him since the moment he gave himself and opened his soul. And today he would use this bully pulpit to spread the joyous news. He became aware of the audience murmuring and looked out at the crowd.

"Friends. Today I stand before you a very different Miles Massey than the man who addressed you last year on the disposition of marital assets following murder slash suicide."

Miles paused to master the emotions stirred by his admission.

"I wish to talk to you today not about technical matters of law. I wish to talk to you about something more important. I wish to talk to you from the heart. Because today, for the first time in my life, I stand before you naked . . . vulnerable . . . and in love."

His statement sparked a low buzz among the attendees. Miles didn't care what they were saying. He hadn't come this far to compromise. He intended to say his piece and damn the consequences.

"Love," Miles said with a bemused smile, "it's a word we matrimonial lawyers avoid. Funny, isn't it—that we are frightened of this emotion which is in a sense the seed of our livelihood." He gazed out at the audience. "But today, Miles Massey is here to tell you: Love need cause us no fear. Love should cause us no shame. Love . . . is good."

Miles saw some of the lawyers in the audience exchange puzzled *is he on drugs?* sort of looks. Others began to cough nervously. He could feel the room curdle like spoiled milk. *The truth always makes people uncomfortable,* he thought, but he plowed on.

"Now I am, of course, aware that these remarks may be received with cynicism." There was a smattering of appreciative laughter. "Cynicism—that refuge of the weak, the selfish, the emotionally paralyzed. Cynicism—that cloak which advertises our indifference and drives away all human feeling. Cynicism—that suit of armor which we poor frightened combatants put on to approach the bar."

Miles looked around, eyes shining. "Well, I am here to tell you that cynicism, which we think protects us, in fact destroys—destroys love, destroys our clients and ultimately—destroys ourselves."

The audience stared as he poured a glass of water and sipped. He took another thoughtful sip. "Colleagues!" Miles said finally. "Let me ask you a question. When our clients come to us confused and angry, hurting because their flame of love is guttering and threatens to die . . ."

Miles paused and looked out at their blank faces. "Should we seek to extinguish that flame, so that we can sift through the smoldering wreckage for our paltry reward?" He let them consider the question.

"Or should we fan this precious flame—this *most* precious flame—back to loving, roaring life? Should we counsel fear or trust? Should we seek to destroy—or to build? Should we meet our clients' problems with cynicism—or with love?"

Miles took a deep breath, smiled and shook his head. "The decision is, of course, each of ours. For my part I have made the leap of love, and there is no going back. Ladies, gentlemen, this is the last time I shall address you as the president of NOMAN—or as a member . . ."

This time the buzzing grew louder. Miles raised his hands and the murmur subsided. "I intend to devote myself hereafter to pro bono work in East Los Angeles, or wherever I am needed. Thank you—and may God bless you all."

Head bowed, Miles turned and began walking across the podium, his shoes squeaking on the wooden floor. There was total silence as he moved past the stunned officers seated in a long row behind the dais. Somewhere there was a lonely cough.

Miles reached the stairs at the end of the podium and started descending. Someone at the rear of the banquet hall began to clap. Slowly, uncertainly, until someone else joined him. By the time Miles hit the bottom step there was a small scattering of sustained applause.

As Miles started up the center aisle the applause grew. One clapping man rose to his feet. More joined him and the applause began to swell louder until it included the entire hall. One man reached out and thumped Miles on the back as he made his way to the exit.

"Thank you, Miles!" someone shouted.

The applause continued to grow and everyone in the audience was on his feet. People near the aisle reached out to lay a congratulatory hand on Miles as he passed. The audience was roaring. Before Miles reached the door he was mobbed by admirers, all reaching out to him. Through the sea of faces he caught someone's eye. He moved forward and the applauding crowd parted.

Wrigley stood there, shaking his head in disbelief.

For a moment the two men stared at each other. Then Wrigley flung open his arms. "I love you, man," he croaked, rushing to embrace Miles.

Around them, the crowd cheered and pounded them both on the back. Wisely, Wrigley hustled Miles through the mob and out of the banquet hall. As they hurried away they could still hear the distant cheers.

Wrigley's glasses were fogged and tears streamed down his face.

"That was your finest hour, Miles," he said simply.

Miles shrugged. "Let's find a drink."

The cocktail lounge at Caesars was located just off the casino floor. It had a red leather bar with high-back stools and a large-screen TV. Normally the TV was turned to some sporting event upon which money could be wagered.

However, since there were very few customers before five, Wolf the bartender and Kate the cocktail waitress followed the soap operas.

Miles and Wrigley were oblivious to everything in the empty lounge as they entered. Wrigley listened in rapt fascination while Miles outlined his plans.

"So Wrigley, I'll be relinquishing my partner-ship in Massey, Myerson," he said cheerfully. "If you would like to join me in my new endeavors, I would be delighted to have you."

Wrigley nodded eagerly. Miles signaled the bartender, who was adjusting the volume on the TV. The announcer's voice drifted louder.

"We return now for the conclusion of today's episode of *The Sands of Time* . . ."

Miles leaned closer to Wrigley. "Of course, I can't offer you the kind of financial remuneration that you've grown accustomed to, but the work will have its own rewards." He looked up. "Barkeep?"

Both the bartender and waitress were engrossed in the TV.

"The patient is suffering from acute myocar-dial infarction—we have to operate!" the TV doctor declared.

"Dr. Howard rules," the waitress said to no one in particular.

Absently, Wrigley glanced up at the screen, his brow furrowed.

"Hey, isn't this the soap that used to belong to Donovan Donnelly?"

Miles ignored the question. "You'll be serving in a junior capacity, of course . . ."

A second doctor came onscreen. "Shouldn't we call in a specialist from Mass General?"

"You don't need a specialist," the waitress answered. "You got Dr. Howard."

"Say Miles," Wrigley said in hushed tones, eyes on the TV. "Isn't that, isn't that . . . ?

Miles continued making his point. "As you know, in any firm there can be only one ramrod—" He paused as Wrigley tugged at his sleeve.

Casually, Miles followed Wrigley's gaze to the TV.

He didn't see it right away. How could he?

It was impossible.

Miles glanced at Wrigley, who kept staring at the screen. Then he looked up again. *It was impossible. Wasn't it?"*

The TV doctor was none other than . . . Howard Doyle.

*Marilyn's ex-husband in now an actor?* Miles wondered, dumbfounded.

He watched with growing agitation as Howard Doyle, dressed in the pale green hospital scrubs of a daytime TV surgeon, handled matters with dignified intensity. Gone was his rube accent and boob manner. Dr. Howard was as cool as Mike Wallace on *60 Minutes.*

"Good God, man, we can't wait for a specialist," Dr. Howard said firmly. "Look at her upper left ventricle—that infarct is dynamite!"

The second doctor shook his head. "But doctor, you're new here—it would be your first procedure here at St. Ignatius and—" he gave Dr. Howard a grave stare "—she's your daughter!"

Dr. Howard shrugged. "Let me tell you what they called me in medical school: Mackenzie the Mechanical Marvel . . ." He solemnly regarded his hands and flexed his fingers. ". . . I've got no nerves."

"Oh, Dr. Howard . . ." The waitress moaned softly.

Unable to speak, to utter the unutterable, Wrigley gaped open-mouthed and pounded on the bar as if he were choking. "He's . . . he's . . ."

Wrigley turned to Miles, gasping like a hooked fish. ". . . An actor! *Not* an oil tycoon. An *actor.*"

Miles nodded, trying to absorb the information.

Adjusting his spectacles, Wrigley weighed the implications. "So that means Marilyn—" he looked at the TV then at Miles "—golly, she has no money. She . . . she's *poor.*"

Miles's unbearable lightness of being evaporated. Suddenly it was all hideously clear. Everything finally fell into place like huge blocks of granite—crushing Miles with the unbearable weight of reality.

Noticing his stricken expression, Wrigley gave his shoulder an encouraging pat. "Well, thank God, you have the prenup."

Miles's stare was that of a mortally wounded gladiator. His eyes seemed to gaze bleakly at Wrigley from the blood-soaked dirt of the arena.

"I have no prenup."

Wrigley nodded and thoughtlessly repeated the unthinkable. "You *have* no prenup."

"I have no prenup. She tore it up."

"She tore it up." It took Wrigley a few moments before it came tumbling down on him. His eyes grew wide with alarm.

"YOU HAVE NO PRENUP?!"

Miles nodded mutely. Then he seemed to realize the enormous horror. His features contorted, lips pulled back in a deathlike grimace and he howled, "AAAAAGGHHHHEEEE!"

"AAAAAGGHHHEEEE!" Wrigley wailed, swept up by primitive emotions.

For the first time the waitress and bartender looked at them.

Miles stood up and his contorted expression

became deadly calm. "Freddy Bender," he said softly.

Before Wrigley could reply, Miles bolted out of the bar and began trotting back toward the banquet hall.

Wrigley noticed the waitress and bartender looking at him. He gave them an apologetic smile and started after Miles.

"Jerks musta won something," the bartender muttered, turning back to the TV.

The waitress shrugged. "Stiffed us on the tip."

Miles headed blindly across the casino floor, not noticing who or what was in his way. One thought drove him, centered his seething emotions to a single savage urge, to strangle Freddy Bender with his bare hands.

Only Freddy could have crafted that phony marriage. And the barbecue sauce on the prenup? That was pure Freddy. He put Marilyn up to this . . . this loathsome travesty.

Unmindful of Wrigley struggling to catch up, Miles charged ahead. Without slowing down he turned toward the banquet hall, scattering a few tourists in his path.

As he neared, Miles had to push through the current of humanity streaming out of the banquet room. Oblivious to the claps on the back from his admiring colleagues, he moved steadily forward, searching the crowd for his quarry.

"You're beautiful, man," one lawyer said.

"We dissolved the society," another told him.

"By acclimation!" a third said proudly.

Miles forged on, propelled by his blood lust and his pain. A pain he didn't yet feel but was there in the form of a vague longing. A sense of loss. Then Miles saw him, standing near the bar. Drinking a martini and laughing. And a hot red curtain fell over his eyes.

"FREDDY!" Miles bellowed, shoving two lawyers out of the way.

At the sound of his name Freddy turned and smiled. The smile froze when he saw Miles rushing at him as if he was holding a football instead of a martini. Before Freddy could run, Miles grabbed his lapels and swung him against the wall.

"I'm going to see that you get disbarred!" Miles rasped breathlessly, his eyes red and his teeth bared. "And prosecuted!" He squeezed the lapels tighter, choking off Freddy's breath. "Thrown into jail!"

Freddy kicked and struggled. "Take your hands off me, Massey."

The others milled around, uncertain of why their love guru was attacking a fellow lawyer.

Freddy started to cough. Miles pulled tighter. "You just wait until I . . ."

Just then Wrigley arrived and grabbed Miles's shoulder. Freddy tried to wrench free but Miles wouldn't let go.

"I've done nothing illegal or unethical," Freddy sputtered, aware of the onlookers.

"You lied!" Miles shouted. "You lied! You said Howard Doyle—"

Freddy rolled his eyes. "They were married. They were divorced," he declared in an exasperated drone reserved for unruly children. "There were no assets. Everything was on the up-and-up. Granted, his accent was phony, but I'm aware of no law against that."

Some of the steam went out of Miles. "AHHHH!" he rasped, releasing Freddy.

"Why did she do it, Freddy?" Miles demanded. "Why?"

It was *the* question of the ages.

Freddy pulled down his sleeves, brushed his suit, then regarded Miles with sphinxlike disdain. "That's attorney-client privilege. Marilyn has retained me to pursue an action in which I believe you will figure as respondent."

*Respondent.* The word ripped his heart like a bullet. *Is that all it comes down to?* Miles asked himself. *The cosmic attraction, the plans for the future, the possibilities of family and future, reduced to dollars and cents? That universal love, that unbelievable night, was all about revenge?*

The answer came back from the depths of his despair.

*Yes.*

Freddy had gathered himself sufficiently to make a dignified exit, leaving Miles to his misery. However, he couldn't resist a bit of a gloat. Considering all he'd endured from Miles. Especially the Guttman case.

"Sorry, Massey, but as a great and clever man once said, 'What's good for the gander . . .' "

Wrigley had to restrain Miles. "Easy. We're lucky he doesn't sue. And he still may."

But Miles wasn't listening. He was thinking about Marilyn. Her last few words she said as he left: *I'll miss you, darling.* They bounced around inside his skull like steel balls in a pinball machine, setting off an array of chaotic emotions. He turned, and started hurrying back to the honeymoon suite.

Wrigley knew where Miles was going. Miles would have to take care of the Marilyn problem on his own, he decided. Wrigley beamed a smile at the postfight stragglers. Meanwhile, he needed to mend some fences.

Miles still couldn't accept the enormity of what

Marilyn had done. Stunned and wounded, he rushed to the elevators and rocked impatiently as he waited to be transported to the penthouse floor. *I'll miss you, darling,* looped around his brain in various shades of meaning.

*Why did she do it?* he kept asking himself. His only answer was the *ding* of the floor bell. When the door slid open, he was met by the bellman, who was wheeling a rack loaded with luggage.

Marilyn's luggage.

Miles stormed into the suite. She was still there, putting some items in a toiletry case. As he came closer the Afghan growled at him.

Marilyn didn't seem surprised. "Oh, hello, Miles. Freddy said you were on your way."

Miles didn't even curse Freddy. His rage, indignation and disgust had all been distilled down to utter desolation. He was devastated.

"Back to Los Angeles?" he asked, trying to sound casual.

"Yes." She gave him a pitying glance. "I think it's only fair to warn you. After a decent interval I plan to have Freddy seek an injunction that will forbid your approach within five hundred feet of my house."

"Meaning *my* house?"

"I believe the residence will be part of the settlement."

*Despite the fact that you never resided there with me,* Miles noted sadly. "Did last night mean anything to you?" he said aloud.

Her smile became playful. "Oh, about the same as it'll mean to you—one half of your net worth." Then her expression softened and she regarded him with something close to fondness.

"You'll always be my favorite husband, Miles," she said, voice husky.

Miles slumped as if he'd been struck with a bat. "Marilyn . . . please!"

*You're begging,* he realized with horror. *Begging like a beaten respondent.* And yet he couldn't stop himself. "Please, let's try—"

"Sorry, darling, no more sentiment." She leaned closer and gave him a peck on the cheek. "I really have to be going. The dog is rented."

Dazed, Miles watched her breeze out of the room. He sat heavily on the bed, aware of an aching sense of loss. He looked over and saw the Afghan had remained behind.

Oddly, the hound was making a snarling face at him as it hunched over. *The dog never liked me,* Miles thought dejectedly.

He heard the crisp sound of Marilyn's voice from the hallway.

"Howard!"

Tail wagging enthusiastically, the Afghan straightened up and bounded away, leaving a dark pile of shit on the thick white rug.

Haunted, Miles stared at the pile of shit, sinking deeper into the murky swamp of total depression. He saw it as a metaphor for his entire life.

# CHAPTER
# SIXTEEN

It was a perfect afternoon in Hollywood.
The sky was clear and the smog hovered way
down at the base of the hills. Higher up, there
was money in the air.

Fresh from a morning of yoga, pilates and
facials, Marilyn and her girlfriend—the very much
alive Sarah Sorkin—were stretched out on the
deck beside Miles's pool. Marilyn's two rottweilers
were also there; one snoozing in the sun, the other
resting his head adoringly on Marilyn's feet.

Outdoor speakers that resembled large rocks
played Edith Piaf singing, *Rien, rien, Je ne regret
rien* . . . while both women gazed contemplatively
at the sparkling surface of the pool. Marilyn

sipped from her fruit and rum drink. Sarah held a glass of Pepto-Bismol.

Marilyn's mind kept drifting back to Miles. His reaction had been unexpected. Unlike most men, he showed no sign of anger or vindictiveness. He seemed genuinely hurt. And judging from the speech he had made in Las Vegas, his love had been equally genuine.

*Euphoria is not love,* Marilyn silently corrected, sipping her drink. Anyway, she had beaten Miles at his own game. Fair and square.

*To the victor go the spoils,* Marilyn reminded. But she wasn't convinced. *So I won. Now what? I'm back at square one. No man, empty life, nothing in my future but patch, patch, patch.*

Marilyn tried to shake off the thought by rolling over on the deck chair. *Why complain? I got what I wanted. I have independence, I have options, use them.* It made perfect sense—but it didn't heal the aching loss, or dispel the haunting idea that she had made a grave mistake.

"Penny . . ." Sarah murmured. "I can feel you brooding from over here."

Marilyn sighed. "Oh, you know . . . Miles, the settlement."

Sarah looked at her carefully. "But you *are* going through with it?"

"Yes, yes, it's just that I felt sorry for him for a minute there. At the preliminary hearing he seemed so . . . *beaten*."

"Well, he *is* beaten," Sarah reminded. "Fair and square." She sat up and rummaged through her bag for a mirror and skin cream.

"Yes, but . . ." *Not really so fair,* she wanted to say.

"Uh-huh, that pathetic look," Sarah said with a knowing smirk. "That's what they fall back on when they don't have a prenup." She looked at Marilyn encouragingly. "Just stay strong until the divorce is final. Relax and enjoy your pool."

*The problem is it doesn't feel like my pool,* Marilyn thought mournfully. *Maybe if I actually take a swim.* She wondered how often Miles used it.

She listened to Edith Piaf and the lapping water, then sighed and looked at Sarah. "Do you think he's eating enough?"

Sarah sat bolt upright. "Marilyn!" she said indignantly.

Marilyn got up and dove into the pool.

It felt wonderful.

Wrigley had been living in fear of this since Las Vegas.

He had been summoned—along with Miles—to Herb Myerson's office. It was the first time since joining the firm that he would actually meet the fabled Herb Myerson face to face. And he wasn't looking forward to it.

Especially given Miles's wretched condition.

Miles had fallen a long way from the exalted peak he had briefly occupied in Vegas. His appearance had deteriorated. He showed up at the office unshaven, hungover, wearing rumpled clothes. But even worse, his brilliant legal mind had gone on vacation. All of his cases had to be postponed or farmed off to lesser attorneys.

Wrigley hated to see his hero's decline. But he hated going to Herb Myerson's office even more.

He had heard rumors about Myerson and his methods. Rumors about what happened to attorneys unfortunate enough to get on Myerson's shit list. Now Miles was on Myerson's shit list. And Wrigley's name would be added after this meeting.

*Guilt by association,* Wrigley reflected darkly. *After all, I am Miles's associate.* He hesitated at the door. *We who are about to die salute you.*

But Wrigley wasn't quite ready for what he saw when he entered.

The venetian blinds were closed and the curtains drawn. The only light came from a desk lamp. Through the gloom, Wrigley saw Miles standing in front of a large mahogany desk. Behind the desk sat a hunched, gray-skinned figure with thick round glasses that made him resemble a mummified owl.

Herb Myerson.

The hunched figure didn't seem to be aware of Wrigley's presence. Nor did Miles.

Wrigley felt queasy. He moved behind Miles as if to hide.

At the moment a stocky nurse was unhooking something from the bottom of Herb Myerson's wheelchair. She removed a plastic bag of yellowish fluid and replaced it with a fresh drainage bag. Then she deftly reattached Myerson's arm to the IV unit.

As the liquid began to drip into Myerson's vein, he began to speak.

"This woman has humbled . . . shamed and disgraced the entire foim." His hoarse rasp slithered through the gloom.

Wrigley felt queasier. He looked at Miles, who stood calmly, hands clasped like a defendant in front of a hanging judge.

"Yes, Herb," Miles said.

"Counseluh, the foim deals in powuh, this foim deals in p'seption. This foim cannot prospuh, nor long endoowa . . . if it is p'seeved as dancin' to the music . . ." Myerson waved his free arm in a ghastly parody of dance.

". . . of the hoidy-goidy."

Wrigley winced, hoping Miles wouldn't try to defend his love-inspired flight to the ivory tower. He was oddly disappointed when Miles didn't.

"I understand, Herb." Miles shook his head. "I just . . . for the first time in my career, I don't know what to do. I'm a patsy. A sitting duck." His voice cracked slightly. "I'm lost."

"Lawst!" Myerson spat the word across his desk, eyes glowing red inside shadowy sockets. "I'll tell you what you can do!"

Wrigley shivered and moved closer behind Miles.

"You can—" Myerson stopped short and pointed a bony finger at the nurse. "Leave us."

Instantly, the nurse gathered her bags and headed for the door. As she came around the desk, Wrigley fell into step behind her. All he wanted in life was to be on the other side of the door.

"Not you, counseluh!"

The raspy voice curled around Wrigley's throat like a noose and yanked him back. Whimpering, he retook his station behind Miles.

"You can act like a man!" Myerson rasped. "Let me tell you sump'n, smart guy. You tawt you had it awl figgud out Trust. Marriage. All ya goddamn love, love, love. Well, now you lissena me. I'm gonna tawk to you about the goddamn *law.*"

The word hushed the room. Wrigley felt a chill go up the back of his neck as the hunched cadaverous figure, leaned forward in his wheelchair, his eyes burning red in the gloom.

Herb Myerson painfully pushed himself to his feet. Even standing he seemed to be seated behind the desk. Slowly, with great difficulty, he began to pace, the IV unit swaying dangerously behind him.

"We SOIVE the law!" he declared, voice trembling with effort. "We HONUH the law! We make our goddamn bread 'n BUTTUH by the law."

Myerson looked at Miles, his parched gray features as impassive as a corpse. "And sometimes, counseluh, we OBEY the law . . ." He paused to let this sink in. ". . . But, counseluh, this is not one a' those times."

Wrigley wondered if he'd heard correctly. Then it became horribly clear.

Myerson's trembling, liver-spotted hand pushed a card across the desk. "This is the num-

-194-

buh of an expoit in these delicate mattuhs. Code name a' Wheezy Joe."

"What do you suggest, Herb?" Miles asked calmly.

"I suggest, counseluh, that you set up a meet and handle it in such a mannuh that will sevuh any and all connections between that numbuh— and this foim," he said, voice puncturing the gloom like an ice pick.

Myerson lowered himself heavily into the wheelchair. "And tell your associate ta toughen up."

Miles picked up the card and walked out, Wrigley a half step behind him. It wasn't until they reached Miles's office that Wrigley fully understood what Herb Myerson had actually advised.

For almost an hour Wrigley tried to get Miles to change his mind.

But his mentor was adamant. "Herb is right on this," he muttered, signaling the bartender. "Don't worry, I've got a bulletproof plan."

Bulletproof. Wrigley hated it already. When the bartender arrived he ordered a screwdriver. They were discussing their next move in the anonymity of the Formosa bar and the place was nearly empty. The afternoon drinkers didn't arrive until four.

"But Miles, you love her," Wrigley pleaded. "You told me yourself."

Miles looked at him, eyes strangely glazed. "I do love her, Wrigley. That's why I have to do this. It . . . comes down to honor. I put my ass on the line for that woman."

"And she nailed it," Wrigley conceded. "But this—"

Miles waved the card. "Is the way to handle it." He leaned closer and whispered in Wrigley's ear. "This comes from Herb himself. Now. . ."

He clapped Wrigley on the shoulder. ". . . toughen up. We have a few details to work out."

"Such as?"

"Names, disguises, cover story—that sort of thing."

Wrigley drained his screwdriver and ordered another. Halfway down the second drink he started to warm up to the plan. Miles was right; if they used phony names, paid cash and wore disguises, there could be no link to them or the firm. By the time he'd finished his drink and ordered another, Wrigley was looking forward to their meet with Wheezy Joe.

He'd show Herb Myerson tough.

Then Wrigley saw Miles get up—card in hand—and walk to the public phone near the rest room. Suddenly his resolution crumbled. The clammy feeling that he was in way too deep slid over him like quicksand.

To his horror, Wrigley realized that Miles was about to call the number. And he was about to become an accessory to murder.

# CHAPTER
# SEVENTEEN

Wheezy Joe was an acquired taste.
By the time a person acquired his number, they had reached a position of some importance. A position they didn't want to lose.

It was something Wheezy Joe counted on in terms of their silence.

When he received the call from Mr. Smith, he immediately knew he was dealing with people of discretion. And for a hit man, discretion was everything.

The only thing Wheezy Joe disliked about his profession was his code name. Like his father, he happened to be an asthmatic. Having followed in the family business he inherited his father's code name.

Wheezy Joe tried to accept it. He fished his plastic inhaler out of the driver's compartment and took a deep hit as he neared the clam house. He parked the Caddy and struggled to extract his three-hundred-and-fifty-pound bulk from the car. When he reached the restaurant he was perspiring through his green silk shirt and breathing noisily through his open mouth. Sweating and wheezing, he entered the dining room and spotted his new clients immediately.

They were seated in a booth, side by side, wearing ridiculous disguises.

The younger one, with the specs, had a black wig and moustache that made him look like a failed Latino pimp. The other one wore the dark glasses and black wool watch cap of an inner-city rapper.

Joe moved to the booth. "Mr. Smith?"

"Are you Wheezy Joe?" the rapper inquired.

Joe sat down. He stared at them, poked the inhaler in his mouth and squeezed. *Whush*. Still staring he removed the inhaler. "Which a youse is Smith?"

The rapper lifted his hand. "Uh . . . we're here *representing* Mr. Smith on a . . . matter of some delicacy."

Joe hadn't gone beyond tenth grade but he

knew a rich mouthpiece when he saw one—or two, in this case. "Who's the pigeon?"

The rapper smiled. He had perfect teeth. "Excuse me?"

This was the part Joe always enjoyed. He watched them intently.

"Who ya want me to kill?"

His new clients stiffened and glanced at each other nervously.

The rapper's smile faded. "Well, uh, we—uh, that is to say, *Mr. Smith* would like to, uh, neutralize a, uh, terminate, uh—render into a state of, uh, you know, so she isn't so much, uh . . ."

". . . Breathing," the pimp offered.

"A certain, uh, business associate by the name of Marilyn Rexroth-Doyle Massey," the rapper said, producing an envelope.

"Is that . . . *one* person?" Joe asked suspiciously.

The rapper slid the envelope across the table. "Here's her picture . . . and your, uh, fee, of course."

Joe hefted the thick envelope. It felt right.

"You'll, uh, also find the address where she's staying, it's the residence of Mr. Massey."

The pimp whispered something.

"Uh . . . Smith," the rapper corrected, completely undone. Uh, Massey . . ." He made an effort to compose himself. "It's, uh, Mr. Smith's house. Though Smith himself is not involved."

The pimp leaned forward. "Because of impending legal action we need this to happen within a certain . . . time frame."

"On an expedited basis," the rapper explained.

As Joe digested the information he studied them. Absently he picked his inhaler, poked it in his mouth and squeezed the plunger. *Whush.*

"You're in a rush," Joe said.

The pimp nodded. "Mr. Smith is, yes."

Joe continued to study them. The rapper seemed more and more agitated. Finally he blurted out, "She won't suffer, will she?"

The rapper bit his knuckle, gazing fearfully at Joe.

Joe shrugged. "Not unless you pay extra."

Later, while consuming a dinner of lasagna, veal, chicken and meatballs, Joe decided the sit-down had gone as well as could be expected. Obviously, his new clients were rank amateurs, but their money was good. *Good thing they ain't in the crime racket,* Joe observed. *They wouldn't last a day. That business with the disguises and Mr. Smith . . .*

Joe wasn't any Einstein, but it was clear that the rapper was this Mr. Massey/Mr. Smith character—and he wanted his wife bumped off for taking his house. Joe could empathize, it was the manly thing.

*Whoever this Smith guy is, he came to the right man,* he thought. Once Wheezy Joe went into action, nothing could stop him from eliminating the problem. Nothing.

He speared a meatball with his fork, and put the inhaler in his mouth.

*Whush.*

Miles was having second, third, and fifth thoughts. He paced around Wrigley's apartment like a caged wolf, swigging tequila from the bottle.

"I don't think I can stand it," he said for the twentieth time. "I'm going to abort."

"Consider the alternatives," Wrigley said, fitting his couch with sheets and blankets. "You lose half your assets but keep all the debt. Then there's alimony. Marilyn didn't get anything from Rexroth—thanks to you. You'll be paying her mortgage on your ex-house. And you never lived there together."

*Now she'll die there,* Miles noted. The thought was agonizing.

"Then there's your credibility. When Freddy spreads the news that you have no prenup . . ."

Wrigley let the answer hang. But they both knew what it meant: professional ridicule, loss of client confidence, the overnight downward spiral for which Hollywood is renowned.

Miles gulped tequila. "I suppose it's the only way."

"She did trick you," Wrigley reminded.

"It was brilliant," Miles said with a wistful smile. His eyes grew misty.

Wrigley regarded the made-up couch. "I hope you'll be comfortable on here."

Miles groaned. "I can't sleep while this is happening—I may never sleep again . . ." He took another pull from the bottle. "How did it go from love to this?"

Wrigley didn't answer. He took the bottle from Miles and had a swig. "You went into it with the best of intentions," he said finally.

Miles grunted agreement. But it didn't ease the gnawing pain. Not even the tequila could do that.

"Do you think he bought it?" Miles asked after a while.

"Who?"

"He—Wheezy Joe."

"Hook, line and sinker," Wrigley assured, patting the couch. "The disguise thing was perfect."

"It was a nice touch." Miles sat heavily on the

edge of the makeshift bed and stretched out. "Go to sleep, Wrigley, I'll just stay up and . . ."

He began to snore.

Ever since his divorce, Rex Rexroth had been living like the raja of railroads. The real estate deal brought him a quick thirty million, which afforded him plenty of time to explore his favorite hobby.

In the process, Rex had moved past Nina, settling her in a cozy condo in Santa Barbara. As his appetites became sated, his curiosity expanded. Wichita Lineman, Night Train, Milk Train, Cannonball Express, Orient Express, Marrakech Express, Theater Car, Club Car, Boxcar; he had played them all with varying numbers of exotic ladies.

Rex had also traveled the world, riding the last of the great rail lines from Paris to Istanbul, Rome to Stockholm, champagne and sex all the way.

*Less than a year ago I was on the brink of annihilation,* Rex reflected, counting his blessings. *Marilyn had my house, my assets, the real estate thing was turning sour. My private life was open to scorn and public ridicule.* Until one man came riding in like the Lone Ranger and saved his ass.

That masked man was Miles Massey, he noted reverently. Rex lifted his glass in a silent toast. Someday he would do something nice for that man.

Meanwhile . . . Rex turned to regard the bevy of beauties cavorting about the large bedroom, partaking of the food and wine buffet. Meanwhile . . . life was very good.

*Maybe too good,* Rex observed, catching his reflection in the mirror. He'd put on some weight lately. His boxcar boxer shorts were cutting into his swelling belly. And lately he'd been bothered by severe indigestion.

Rex didn't let it cramp his style. He added cocaine to his champagne and steak diet, which did away with the discomfort and stimulated his imagination.

In a rush of creative energy Rex had remodeled his enormous, oak-paneled bedroom. It was now the Pullman Room. The chairs, sofas and huge circular bed were upholstered in crimson crushed velvet, and a coal fire roared in one corner. The sole modern touch was the large screen above the bed.

Soft-porn images of naked ladies flickered across the screen, intercut with vintage train footage of various locomotives, signalmen in overalls waving lanterns, trains pulling into stations or crossing majestic landscapes.

Rex popped a Viagra, washed it down with champagne, took a sniff of coke and hurried to rejoin his naked beauties.

"Okay ladies, let's take it from the top," he said, jumping on the bed. "Coal stokers front and center." He put on his engineer cap.

The girls squealed with delight. At five hundred bucks an hour they were having the time of their lives. There were six of them, their creamy white bodies smeared with coal dust. As Rex began to sing they danced around the bed.

"*I've* been workin' on the railroad . . . !" Rex bellowed.

"All the live long day!" the girls sang back.

Rex felt the sweet rush building inside him like a locomotive getting up a head of steam. Oh yes, he was chugging now. He was steaming for the big tunnel like old Sixty-Six.

"*I've* been workin' on the railroad . . . !" he hollered.

"Just to pass the time away!" the ladies chirped.

The rush expanded and Rex felt himself being swept up in the roaring pleasure of a railroad man. He was John Henry, Casey Jones . . . Joel McRae . . . he was comin' 'round the mountain! Comin' 'round the mountain when he comes . . .

"*Can't* you hear the whistle . . . ?" Rex suddenly ran out of steam.

"Can't you hear . . . ?" A bolt of pain shot down Rex's left arm. ". . . The whistle blow—AAAAAGHHH!"

His naked chorus gaped silently as Rex clutched his arm, eyes bulging, and buckled over. Those six coal-smeared tarts were the last things he saw before his heart exploded like an overheated engine.

For a moment the ladies stood there on tiptoe, like soot-smudged fairies poised for flight. Finally one of them stepped forward.

"Whatsa matter, Rexie?" she said cautiously.

Rexie grinned up at her as if he had a secret. Seconds later the secret was out. Rex was deader than the Twentieth Century.

# CHAPTER
# EIGHTEEN

The monstrous gray figure was stalking him, trailing a long curly wire jacked into his frail arm like a phone cord. Miles kept running but every time he stopped, the hunched figure would emerge from the fog . . . coming closer . . . bony fingers wriggling like white tarantulas . . .

A distant alarm began to ring. It rang again and Miles dimly realized he'd been having a nightmare. On the third ring he realized it was a phone in another room.

Slowly Miles started to remember. Wrigley's apartment.

He clapped the pillow over his head and dove back into sleep. Even the nightmare was better than reality. Despite his attempt to block

out the world, Miles could hear Wrigley's muf-
fled voice.

"Hello? . . . yes, he's here. Just a minute."

Miles waited, counting the seconds of blessed
oblivion before Wrigley entered. "Miles? It's for
you . . . urgent."

Moaning with the effort, Miles pulled away
the pillow, squinting against the light Wrigley
had stupidly switched on.

Wrigley was taken aback. This wasn't the Miles
he knew. This Miles was bleary-eyed, unshaven,
uncombed, disheveled and uncertain. He took
the offered phone with an unsteady hand.

"Hello . . . yes . . . *what?*" Miles sat up, the fog
clearing from his face. "Yes . . . I see, thank you."
He sat for a few moments, phone pressed against
his ear. Then he let the instrument tumble to the
floor.

"My God . . ." Miles said hoarsely.

Wrigley's brow furrowed with concern.
"What?"

"That was Marvin Untermeyer."

"Yes?"

"He was Rex Rexroth's personal attorney."

"Ye—what do you mean *was?*"

Miles stared bleakly into empty space, his
voice flat. "Rex just had a massive coronary—in
the middle of a business meeting. He's dead."

Wrigley looked at him. Miles seemed to be devastated by the news. He sat slumped on the couch, staring straight ahead.

Somewhat puzzled, Wrigley said, "Well, I'm sorry to hear that. But you weren't that close, were you?"

Miles continued to stare into space. "Martin says that Rex's will is four years old," he said woodenly. "He never redrafted it."

Wrigley blinked. "Yes?"

Miles's voice remained flat and toneless, like a man who'd just enjoyed shock therapy.

"Everything goes to Marilyn."

The words hung in the air, arcing like a fishing line. Wrigley tried to grasp their meaning. Miles looked at him.

When their eyes hooked up, Wrigley understood. It was all going horribly wrong. They would all be executed for an unnecessary crime.

"AGGHGHHHHHHHHH!" Miles howled.

"AGGHGHHHHHHHHH!" Wrigley shrieked.

Miles pushed himself to his feet. "Coffee!"

Wrigley rushed to the kitchen while Miles paced back and forth, trying to pump air into a brain that felt like a deflated soccer ball left out in the rain too long.

*Marilyn is rich, there's no need for Wheezy Joe,* Miles speculated. *That's a good thing. But Marilyn happens to be in mortal danger,* he reminded himself as Wrigley brought him coffee. *Wheezy is still on the job—and that's a very bad thing.*

"Wrigley, get me Wheezy's number right away," he said, chugging down his coffee.

"Wheezy Joe?"

"Yes. Hurry up."

Wrigley looked around, patting the pockets on his robe as if he forgot something. "I hid it."

"Well, get it. Now Wrigley. Now."

Wrigley hurried into the bedroom and returned with a small notebook. "Okay, okay, it should be in here."

Miles grabbed the phone. "Shoot."

"Uh," Wrigley peered at the scribbles. "Six, one, one, oh, seven . . ."

As Wrigley called the numbers, Miles dialed with his thumb. His other hand grasped the coffee cup, from which he took trembling slurps.

". . . oh, six." Wrigley completed.

"Seven, oh, six. That's only six digits!" Miles muttered impatiently.

"OH! OH!" Wrigley shouted.

"Seven, oh, six, oh?"

"Oh, seven, oh, six," Wrigley said through clenched teeth.

"Oh, seven, oh, six." Miles started to repunch the numbers, heartbeat revving on a combination of caffeine and raw fear.

"She's not poor," Wrigley said as if he just got the picture. "She's *richer* than you. No prenup. She's exposed. *She's* the sitting duck."

Miles punched the numbers again. "Sitting duck! Yes. Can't kill her! No need!" he said, breathless.

"It would be pointless," Wrigley agreed. "She's exposed."

Miles was beyond reason as he frantically tried again. "Exposed! Pointless— Ahhh!"

"What?"

"Ringing! It's—"

Wrigley moved closer to the phone and heard an answering machine pick up. He heard labored breathing as if someone had run to answer. And then:

"You have reached Wheezy Joe. Wuddya want?" There was more labored breathing before the *beep*.

"Joe!" Miles said frantically. "This is Mr. Mass—Mr. Smith! On Smith's behalf." He glanced at Wrigley, who nodded encouragingly. "Speaking on my own behalf, this is to instruct you it's a NO GO! Do you understand me? No go on Marilyn. This comes directly from Mr. Smith."

Wrigley waved at him. "Although you acknowledge no association," he whispered.

"I—that's right! I acknowledge no association. In connection with this whole affair, which is now no go! But I believe those would be Mr. Smith's wishes." He looked at Wrigley. "Speaking without knowledge."

Miles slammed the phone down. "You think I'm protected?"

"That was good!" Wrigley told him.

"Am I *protected*?"

Wrigley nodded thoughtfully. "I think that would hold up." It suddenly occurred to him that Miles was using his phone. Wrigley felt the queasiness coming up with the coffee.

Miles pointed at him, eyes wide with sudden panic. "Marilyn!"

"Marilyn, yes!" Wrigley said, somewhat confused.

Miles looked around the room as if expecting to find her. "What do we do?" He turned to Wrigley. "What if he's—" He stopped as if unwilling to utter the thought.

Still confused, Wrigley urged him on. "Yes! Yes! What if . . . ?"

"If he's already on his way there?"

Wrigley stood stunned as Miles grabbed his car keys and wallet. "He's—yes! Marilyn!" he said lamely, watching Miles head for the door. "Uh, we, uh, we . . ." Wrigley hurried after him.

He wanted to remind Miles they were both wearing pajamas, but it was too late.

Wheezy Joe had a professional code.

Once he took a contract he didn't stop until the job was finished. That was the deal. Joe reached beside him for the inhaler as he guided the Caddy off the freeway exit. He poked the plastic tube in his mouth and squeezed the plunger. *Whush.*

"Message," Joe said aloud.

The cell phone went into action, dialing his answering machine and signaling a playback. Breathing heavily, Joe listened to Miles's frantic call.

*The guy's got buyer's remorse,* Joe speculated. *Happens alla time.* Can't run a business that way. Wheezy Joe ain't no marriage counter. You make a contract, that's it. Fuggedabowdit.

It being along the way, Joe stopped at a convenience store for an air freshener, Twinkies, a salami sandwich and cleaning gloves. *People wouldn't think it, but you need to be neat in this line of work,* Joe noted, unwrapping the gloves in the car. The short walk inside had taxed his breathing. He reached for his inhaler. *Whush.*

Before he started the Caddy he checked his file. The folder contained the pigeon's picture, address and gate code. *Nice-lookin' broad,* he mused. *The bitch shouldna took the guy's house. Too bad.*

For the rest of the drive Joe played a Johnny Mathis CD followed by Vic Damone. He parked the Caddy some distance from the house and reached for the inhaler. *Whush.* Then he took his Glock nine from the special compartment under the dash and screwed the silencer into the barrel. Before he left the car he touched the statue of the Virgin Mary on his dashboard. Then he slipped on the cleaning gloves, picked up the Glock, put the inhaler in his pocket and rolled his huge girth out of the Caddy.

Halfway to the gate Joe had to stop. *Whush.*

By the time he punched in the security code, Joe was sweating under his shirt. His hands, too, were steaming inside the gloves. His breathing came in slow ragged gasps as he opened the gate and started up the driveway.

When he reached the front door, he paused to listen. Silence.

*Whush.*

Using the code, Joe opened the front door and stepped into the darkened hall. He saw a light leaking out from under a closed door. Joe moved toward the light, floor creaking under his weight. He stopped again and heard his wheezing but saw nothing through the shadows.

Satisfied he had gone undetected, Joe launched his bulk toward the door. The floorboards creaked, making him wish he had worn sneakers.

Just before he reached the door it swung open.

The pigeon was standing in the doorway. She was holding a phone.

Joe lifted the automatic.

# CHAPTER
## NINETEEN

Wrigley had never driven so fast.

He cornered his Saab like a Ferrari as Miles rocked in the seat beside him, doggedly punching numbers into his cell phone.

"Get her out, buy some time," he muttered, wind whipping his pajamas, "get her out, buy some time, get her out—"

He glanced at Wrigley. "She might be out."

"Keep trying!" Wrigley kept his eyes on the narrow tunnel of light dug by his headlamps as he careened around the dark hills. "The machine's not on, she might be sleeping."

Miles tapped the numbers. "Get her out, buy some time, get her out, buy some time," he kept repeating. "Get her out, bu . . . ohmigod, MARI-

LYN! You're there." He made a fist and shot Wrigley an amazed look as if he'd just scored the winning basket.

"Listen, you must leave the house immediately," Miles shouted. "It's imperative that you—"

"Miles?" Marilyn said calmly. "Is that you?"

"Yes! It is imperative that you—"

Marilyn's tone became exasperated. "Oh, please. Miles, pending final settlement, my entitlement to use the house is quite clear . . ."

"You don't undertand . . ."

"Tell her she has to get out," Wrigley hissed.

Miles gave him a warning glare.

". . . In fact," Marilyn continued, "Freddy's restraining order forbids you to even *call me*. So unless there's some kind of emergency . . ."

Miles jumped in his seat. "Yes! That's it! An emergency!"

"An emergency!" Wrigley congratulated.

"What do you mean?" Marilyn asked suspiciously. "What is it?"

"It's . . . it's . . . it's a gas main! Leaking!"

Wrigley gave him a thumbs-up.

"I just remembered I left on the gas main, which leaks!" Miles explained. "Very dangerous! Very!"

"Leaking gas?" Marilyn seemed skeptical.

He lowered his voice, trying to sound alarmed but competent. "A deadly, colorless, odorless, liquidless gas that—that, uh, that attacks the central nervous system and causes diarrhea and facial tics."

"Well—why don't you call the gas man?"

It was the hundred-million-dollar question.

Miles took a deep breath. "Gas man? Like to! Should! Want to! Can't! Can't call the gas man!" He looked around the car searching for inspiration. He saw a safety pin in the cup holder. "Pinned down! Can't get to a phone!"

"You can't get to a phone?" Her tone was part disbelief, part admiration.

Miles spotted a pair of muddy hiking boots in the back. "Camping!" he yelled triumphantly. "I'm camping. Wanted to call the gas man but there's a bear outside my tent."

"Brown bear," Wrigley corrected. An avid hiker, he was somewhat of an expert in sylvan lore.

"*Brown* bear," Miles told her.

"Who's there with you?"

*Doesn't miss a thing,* Miles thought. "No one!" he said quickly. "Wrigley. Also camping—and refuses to make a break for it. Heh, heh—you know Wrigley."

Miles avoided Wrigley's stare of pure hatred.

"So you must leave the house! Immediately!" he said urgently. "Very dangerous."

Marilyn tried to reconstruct his story. "You can't get to a phone to call the emergency gas man because you and Wrigley are pinned down by a bear, so—"

"*Brown* bear."

"—Brown bear," Marilyn said with exaggerated patience. "So you called me up to warn me."

"Exactly! Yes!" Miles shouted. "It's complicated!"

"Well . . ."

"I know what you're thinking," Miles assured. "We've, uh, left out some things for, uh, legal reasons, but it's dangerous. Leave the house!"

Miles disconnected. "I think she bought it."

"Good," Wrigley said. "We're good. What now?"

"We, uh, when we get there we just wait. She'll have left. We wait for Wheezy Joe. We tell him it's a no go."

"Good plan! Good plan!"

"It's done," Miles said, taking a deep breath. "We're protected. I think she bought it."

"Good plan."

"Turn left up here at the stoplight," Miles said.

"But Miles, your house is—"

"Left!"

Wrigley braked hard and half skidded into a left turn. "Where are we going?"

"Seven-Eleven just up the road. Stop there."

Wrigley did as Miles directed, turning into the parking lot.

"Keep the motor running," Miles said. He left the car and trotted into the store. Three minutes later he came out with a paper bag.

"What's in the bag?" Wrigley asked, gunning the car back on the road.

Miles looked grimly ahead. "Ammunition."

Marilyn stood in the half-light holding the phone.

Miles's story was, of course, absurd. But the warning wasn't.

What she couldn't figure out was why. In many ways Miles was a mystery to her. Still, he had called to warn her. That was something.

*Not enough*, she told herself. *Not when it comes to something as serious as this.*

Marilyn moved to the table and picked up a framed photograph of Miles. She studied it for a few moments. *How could he?*

Marilyn heard the sound of labored breathing behind her. The wheezing became louder.

She turned and saw the Fat Man pressed

against the wall, hands raised in surrender. Standing at snarling attention directly in front of him were her two rottweilers. Every once in a while one of the dogs would snap at the Fat Man's leg.

Marilyn approached the Fat Man. She hefted the gun he dropped when the dogs attacked. The Fat Man didn't move. He didn't even look at her. Except for his labored wheeze, he might have been a statue of Buddha.

"Who sent you?" Marilyn demanded.

The man didn't answer.

"They'll attack if I say so."

"Mr. Smith," the Fat Man said. "Mr. Smith sent me."

Marilyn showed the photograph of Miles to the Fat Man. "Is this Mr. Smith?"

"No . . ."

Marilyn prodded him with the gun.

". . . that's his lawyer," the Fat Man said.

The confirmation stung. Marilyn's first reaction was to sting back.

"Well, whatever they're paying you, I'll double it." She looked at the dogs. "Siegfried. Roy."

The rottweilers reluctantly backed up.

The Fat Man took an inhaler from his pocket.

"Who's the pigeon?"

A car screeched to a halt outside.

"That's the pigeon," Marilyn said softly.

The Fat Man took the gun from her hand. "Better you wait upstairs somewhere."

*Whush.*

Before they left the car, Miles reached into the paper bag and gave Wrigley an aerosol cannister of The Mailman's Friend pepper spray.

"Careful," he said hoarsely, "rottweilers."

Still clad in their pajamas, they left the car and started for the darkened house. It seemed deserted. Miles felt certain Marilyn had taken off when he called.

"Stay down," Miles whispered.

Wrigley duckwalked a few feet until he felt a twinge in his lower back. He tried to straighten up but it was difficult. He tried to stay close to Miles, who could navigate in the darkness.

Miles held up a key and pointed at the front door.

Despite his discomfort, Wrigley admired Miles's competence at breaking and entering.

Just before inserting the key, Miles made sure Wrigley had his aerosol can at the ready. It was so quiet that Wrigley could hear the scrape when Miles turned the key. The door swung open on a dark foyer.

Miles tiptoed inside, then motioned for

Wrigley to follow. Painfully aware of his newly acquired back problem, Wrigley stepped inside the house, aerosol can aimed at the darkness.

"I think she's gone," Miles said quietly. He peered through the gloom then smiled at Wrigley. "I think she bought it."

"Oh yeah." Wrigley nodded. "This place is empty." But they were still standing in the foyer.

He followed Miles into the huge living room. For a moment they stood there listening for any strange sounds, such as scrambling rottweilers hunting down intruders.

"Still looks empty," Wrigley whispered.

Miles lifted his aerosol can. "Except for the rottweilers."

"Sure!" Wrigley said, alarmed by the reminder. "Rottweilers." With his stiff back he was in no position to fend off attack dogs.

They crossed the living room and paused. Miles pointed to the door on the right. "Dining room," he whispered. "You check here, I'll do the kitchen." He moved off before Wrigley could protest.

*It's different prowling someone's house alone,* Wrigley noted, moving cautiously to the large door. His back was getting worse, so he was forced to move in a semicrouch, which in this line of work seemed appropriate.

He entered the dining room, which seemed darker still, and began circling the large table, spray can ready.

*It's empty, it's empty,* Wrigley repeated under his breath, but he knew it was wishful thinking. Marilyn had been on the phone not ten minutes before. She might have called the police, she might be hiding with a gun, the rottweilers could be under the table; Wrigley ran through the possibilities as he inched through the shadowy room trying to avoid the breakfront, and various pieces of glassware strewn about like land mines.

Then he heard something. The noise was close by.

Wrigley could hear his heart skipping like a tap dancer.

In the dark he couldn't tell exactly what direction the sound had come from, so he circled slowly. He took a careful step back, another, and started to turn.

Something hard punched his shoulder.

It was like a knife puncturing a grenade. Wrigley exploded in a rush of fear and flight. Then he felt a hand on his face and his back go out at the same time. Paralyzed with fright and pain, Wrigley lifted his spray can and screamed.

# CHAPTER
## TWENTY

Miles was used to raiding the kitchen in his pajamas but usually the lights were on. And he didn't have to worry about strange dogs. He entered the kitchen and stopped, listening for any strange sounds.

It was quiet. Except for a rustling sound, like wind through an open window. He considered opening the fridge to allow more light, but realized it would only make him an easy target.

*Okay, thing to do is take it by quadrants,* he thought, trying to remember a SWAT team training film he had seen on the tube. He began with the oven area on his right. Nothing there. He circled to his left. Empty. *That leaves only ninety percent of the room,* he silently speculated, moving forward through the thick darkness.

The rustling sound grew louder. It was oddly familiar, but he couldn't remember if it was the curtains or something else. He took a careful step forward. The rustle was in front of him and it sounded like . . .

Instinctively, Miles backed away. His shoulder hit the swinging door that separated kitchen from dining room—it swung open six inches and hit something.

Something human.

As Miles turned, he heard a horrifying shriek.

"AAAAEEEEEEEEEE!"

"AAAAEEEEEEEEEE!" he screamed and fogged the air in front of him with pepper spray. At the same time his eyes were seared by a hot mist. Eyes squeezed shut against the burning pain, Miles charged forward—and hit another human.

"AAAAEEEEEEEE," the human howled.

"AAAAAEEEEEEEE," Miles yelled. He spun around and blindly stumbled ahead, eyes tearing and gasping for breath. Suddenly he bumped into what felt like a human chest. A very large human.

*Either that or I ordered an extra freezer,* Miles thought, blinking furiously to clear his sight.

He squinted, and his blurred vision made out

an immense figure. It took him a moment to recover his breath, but his heart was bouncing like a golf ball on concrete.

Then his vision cleared and he made out the huge man's face.

"AHHHHH!" Miles cried, as if greeting a rich uncle. "Wheezy Joe!"

Still dazed, he patted Joe appreciatively on his massive chest. "Thank God you're in time," he rasped. He paused and shook his head. *"You're* not in time. *We're* in time."

As if on signal, Wrigley appeared in the background, his red face and puffy eyes mute testimony to Miles's accuracy.

Wheezy Joe stared at Miles, unmoving. His eyes were as blank as two meatballs in a mound of pizza dough. His breath came in ragged gasps. Like the rustling sound Miles heard in the darkness.

"It's a no go!" Miles told him enthusiastically. "You get it, right? No one any wiser." He made a cow-herding motion with his hands. "You can go home now! Good-bye, thanks so much!"

Wheezy Joe took a pair of earplugs from his pocket.

"No, no! No contract! It's all over! No go!" Miles shouted as Joe carefully twisted the plugs in his ears.

Exasperated he turned to Wrigley. "Wrigley!

Will you explain to this lunkhead!" He turned back and smiled at Joe. "No go! It's all over!"

Wrigley moved face to face with Wheezy Joe. "No go!" he shouted. "No go!"

"We'll settle your contract later!" Miles added. "Big exit bonus."

"Golden parachute!" Wrigley brayed like a game show announcer.

Neither of them noticed that the big man had pulled a large automatic from his pocket.

"Don't you get it!" Miles yelled when Joe refused to move. "It's all off."

Wrigley stepped in front of him. "Here's what happened, Mr. Wheezy . . ."

"It's all off!" Miles repeated, waving his arms. "Look—you're fired! Tornare a Sorrento! Adios, amigo! It's—it's—oh my God!"

Miles stared in horrified disbelief as Wheezy Joe slowly lifted the .45 and pointed it directly at him. Without thinking, he lifted the aerosol and sprayed The Mailman's Friend directly into Wheezy Joe's face.

*Blam!* Eyes scrunched shut, Joe fired but Miles had scurried away.

*Blam!* Sucking for breath like a jet revving for takeoff, Joe fired again.

Miles dove for cover under the table. Wrigley followed, stiff back miraculously cured.

*Bam!* Wheezy Joe lurched around the room, firing his .45 and slapping his pockets for the inhaler. He found it in his righthand pocket. He switched the gun to his left hand and fired again.

*Bam!* Unused to holding the Glock in his left hand, the gun nearly jumped out of his palm. Wheezy Joe grabbed the inhaler with his right hand. Abruptly he began to sneeze. Again he began to struggle to breathe and the lack of air made him dizzy.

Dazed, Joe tried to switch the .45 back to his gun hand—but he bobbled the inhaler. He reached out with the gun to keep the inhaler from falling. Suddenly a blurry image of Miles popped up in front of him. Lungs on fire, Wheezy Joe grabbed for the inhaler.

Frantically he pointed the inhaler at Miles and poked the gun in his mouth.

*Whush.*

Miles squinted through the asthma mist in time to see what was happening.

"WHEEZY JOE!" he shrieked, but it was too late.

Bam! Wheezy Joe left a big hairy red stain on the wall when he collapsed.

Silence.

Wrigley moved to Miles's side. Both men stood in the lingering smoke and pepper spray staring down at Wheezy Joe's body. The gun was still in his mouth but a good portion of his head was missing.

Wrigley shook his head sadly. "We *told* him it was a no go—"

Miles barely heard him. *Where did Wheezy Joe get the idea of shooting me instead?* he wondered.

Miles knew, but he didn't want to believe.

# CHAPTER
# TWENTY-ONE

**M**iles continued to ask that question for many sleepless nights.

*Where had Wheezy Joe gotten the idea to shoot me instead?*

He knew, of course. *Tit for tat,* he told himself. *What's good for the goose* . . . but it saddened him a bit to think hit men had no honor.

It grieved Miles more that he had no honor, as well. He'd been fairly deceived by Marilyn. Wheezy Joe was his fault. He couldn't blame Marilyn for turning the tables.

Marilyn. He took a deep breath. *She's every inch a woman,* Miles thought ruefully. *We belong together. And I've lost her forever.*

Miles stared bleakly through his office window

at the magnificent view of the Hollywood Hills. *Today is the first day of the last day of my life.*

Wrigley sat behind him, playing absently with his fingers. A fruit and pastry basket stood at attention in the center of the conference table. Everything was ready for the execution.

The only sound was the faint whir of the ventilation system.

The intercom broke the gloomy silence. "They're here, Mr. Massey."

Miles let out a small moan and got to his feet. Wrigley got up, as well.

"Dum, dum, da, dum, da dum," Wrigley hummed nervously. The click of the door cut his song short.

Marilyn strode into the room looking as fresh as sunrise; calm, chic and beautiful as ever. Right behind her was Freddy Bender radiating confidence. He placed his attaché case on the tabletop and unsnapped the clasps.

"Gentlemen," Freddy said briskly.

"Freddy," Wrigley greeted.

Miles held a chair for Marilyn. "Hello, Marilyn," he said quietly.

"Hello, Miles."

The tension between them was as thick as pudding as she sat down.

"This . . ." Miles paused. It was difficult to say

what he meant. ". . . This is where we met—remember?"

Marilyn's expression softened. "Of course, I remember."

Miles looked away and sadly shook his head. "Hard to believe that when you go through that door today, you'll be leaving my life forever."

"It's not something . . . I wanted, either," she said softly.

Wrigley was starting to get misty. He watched them both with rapt anticipation. Then Miles went off key.

"But then—I guess something inside me died when I realized you'd hired a goon to kill me," he said through clenched teeth.

Marilyn's eyes widened with indignation. "Wait a minute—*you'd* hired him to kill me!"

Freddy and Wrigley started slapping the table in sudden alarm.

"Now you both wait a minute!" Freddy said sharply. "Nobody hired anyone to kill anyone."

"Hear, hear," Wrigley said, looking at Miles. But he was staring at Marilyn with a vaguely wistful expression. Wistful or pathetic, Wrigley couldn't decide.

Marilyn, on the other hand, was cool and self-composed. Too cool, perhaps. Wrigley really couldn't say. For a moment she seemed ready to try. *Why did Miles have to go there?* he wondered, disappointed. *Everything had been going so well.*

Freddy broke the uncomfortable silence. "Apparently, from what I can gather, a burglar broke into your house—"

"Miles's house!" Wrigley reminded. Everyone looked at him with annoyance.

*"Whatever!"* Freddy rasped. "A burglar broke in intending to loot the place, repented, became despondent over his lifestyle and shot himself."

Miles didn't seem to hear. He was still looking at Marilyn.

"Where does that leave you and me?" he asked quietly.

Freddy flourished a piece of paper. "We've outlined a settlement . . ." He pushed the paper across the table. ". . . we think it's generous."

Miles ignored the paper, which lay unclaimed beside the fruit and pastry basket. He leaned closer to Marilyn but she avoided his eyes.

"My client is prepared to consider a reconciliation!" Wrigley declared before Miles could say something stupid again.

Marilyn looked at Miles, her face clouded with pain. "How could I trust you after . . . all of this?"

"Well, that is exactly right," Freddy interjected hastily. "The point here is that flagrant bad faith has been dem—"

Miles cut him off, his eyes still on Marilyn. "You wounded me first, Marilyn. I'm not proud of what I've done," he added, voice husky with emotion. "But God knows, I did trust you once—and if you give me a chance . . ."

"Heh-heh," Freddy chuckled like a parent at a school play. He looked at Wrigley. "If you'll pardon me, I think my client is well beyond the point of considering any—"

Marilyn paid no attention. "But how could I trust you, Miles? How could I ever really . . ."

Slowly, with his eyes locked on Marilyn, Miles reached into his suit coat. He fished out a piece of paper and laid it flat in front of him, all the while keeping his gaze fixed on Marilyn.

"You know . . . there's nothing in the Massey prenup that says it can't be executed *after* the parties wed." He gave his ballpoint pen a decisive click, looked down at the paper in front of him and scribbled his name.

Miles pushed the paper across the table to Marilyn. Wrigley held his breath, his eyes welling up, but he dared not break the spell by making a sound.

She gazed deeply at him, seeking the truth in his eyes. Absently she picked up the paper. For a long time no one spoke. The only sounds were the hum of the ventilation system and Wrigley's sniffling.

Freddy moved behind Marilyn and leaned over her shoulder, looking down his nose through his glasses at the paper in her hand. However, Marilyn was looking only at Miles.

Wrigley wished he had a camera to record the moment forever. They both seemed so in love with each other.

"Well, if this is indeed the Massey prenup," Freddy said finally, "and a cursory examination tends to suggest that it is—then we withdraw our proffered settlement and there's nothing left to discus—AAAHHHH!"

Freddy gaped horrified as Marilyn deliberately tore the Massey prenup in half and tossed the pieces on the table.

Unable to contain his happiness, Wrigley began sobbing openly. Freddy kept staring at the torn strips of paper.

"My God—Marilyn," Freddy said, voice hushed as if regarding a corpse. "You're . . . you're *exposed!*"

Miles slowly rose to his feet. Marilyn did the same. Miles leaned forward, took her in his arms and kissed her.

Through his tears, Wrigley suddenly noticed something and stopped.

A hand had reached across the table, pinned the torn pieces of paper with two fingers and was furtively dragging them along the tabletop toward himself.

"COUNSELOR!" Wrigley shouted. He dove across the table and—*whack*—slammed his hand down to trap the document.

Too late.

Freddy snatched up the strips of paper and stuffed them into his attaché case. Then, hugging the case to his chest like a football, he scuttled around the table, put a juke move on Wrigley and made a run for the door.

"Come back with that, Counselor!" Wrigley yelled, in hot pursuit.

Miles and Marilyn slowly separated, lost in each other's eyes. Miles took a deep breath, mind and body transformed into a singing instrument.

"Did you hear something?" he murmured.

She sighed. "Only the patter of little lawyer's feet."

"There is something I'd like to know," Miles said, nuzzling her ear. "How did you come up with Howard Doyle?"

"The actor? Oh, through a TV producer." She gave him a playful smile. "I think you know him."

That little cat smile always worried Miles. But he no longer cared. He was no longer afraid of the vagaries of time and love. *So I might get hurt,* he mused, pulling her closer. *So what? Love is a contact sport.*

They kissed again and Miles felt their souls fuse. It was truly a sublime moment. Marilyn put her head against his chest. "I gave that TV producer an idea for a new show," she said lazily. "So he made me a partner."

He kissed her again. "I guess that means I'm a partner."

"I guess it does," she purred.

As Miles leaned in for another kiss, something occurred to him. "What exactly am I partners in?"

She gave him a playful smile. "The premiere airs in four weeks."

This time he wasn't worried.

# EPILOGUE

The show was a hot ticket.

The premiere's success created major buzz around L.A. and every time it aired the studio was packed. The audience represented a number of segments, from industry professionals to neighborhood louts usually seen at *The Jerry Springer Show*.

The air of expectancy grew as the house lights went up and the announcer cupped one ear and called into the mike, "Good evening, ladies and gentlemen, and welcome to *America's Funniest Divorce Videos*."

There was a round of applause.

"And here's the star of our show, Gus . . . FETCH!"

The studio audience roared as Gus Fetch trotted out from behind the curtain. He was wearing a Botany 500 blazer and his trademark porkpie hat. He twisted his bulldog features into his patented nasty grin.

"You're goddamn right, folks, my name is Gus Fetch and we've got a great show for ya."

Gus punched the air with his fist. "We're gonna make you laugh, we're gonna make you weep, and most of all . . ."

Gus waved one arm in a circle over his head leading the audience in a roaring cry. "We're gonna NAIL . . . YOUR . . . ASSSSSSS!!!"

The show's theme music began to play as the house TV monitors showed crude handheld videos of sinning couples caught in flagrante delicto. The money shots.

The show's producer, wearing headphones, kept giving big two-handed upward waves to the audience to cue louder cheers. He clapped his hands to encourage them to do likewise, and energetically pointed at a flashing applause sign.

It was Donovan Donnelly, back from the island of lost producers.

Donovan gave a thumbs-up to his coproducer, working the other side of the stage. Miles Massey grinned back.

Miles was a happy man. He had a new wife and

a new career. He had chucked big-time divorce law and the ghost of Herb Myerson for the most fulfilling profession he had ever known. Coproducer of a hit TV show carried quite a lot of weight in Hollywood; courtside tickets to the Lakers, only two rows away from Jack, permanent reservations at Wolfgang's, an engraved humidor at the Havana Club and a parking spot at the studio.

Miles clapped his hands and grinned at Marilyn sitting in the front row. He was living the dream . . .

On the other side of the stage Donovan watched Miles through narrowed eyes, as if taking aim with a rifle. As fate would have it, his most hated enemy had become his coproducer.

Donovan hadn't forgotten how Miles had taken away his home, his money and his most cherished possession—his award-winning soap opera *The Sands of Time*. He hadn't forgotten that funky pied-à-terre in paradise alley, either.

*Oh no*, Donovan fumed, watching Miles mug for the audience. *The bastard knows how to charm a jury*, all right, Donovan conceded. *But he's on my turf now. There are rules in a court of law. But this is network television. Here the law of the jungle applies. And in this jungle I am an alpha predator. Top of the food chain. I will wait, I will watch, and sooner or later . . . I will nail his ass.*

Miles felt a wave of love from the audience wash over him.

He flashed his nuclear grin and they yelled his name.

*God, I love show business,* he thought.